B+

W9-BGQ-597

RETURN TO PHANTOM HILL

Also by Wayne Barton
In Thorndike Large Print

RIDE DOWN THE WIND

RETURN TO PHANTOM HILL

Wayne Barton

Thorndike Press • Thorndike, Maine

Library of Congress Cataloging in Publication Data:

Barton, Wayne.
 Return to Phantom Hill.

 1. Large type books. I. Title
[PS3552.A777R4 1987]   813'.54   87-40000
ISBN 0-89621-784-1 (alk. paper)

Large Print edition available by arrangement with the author.

Cover design by James B. Murray.

For Margie

CHAPTER 1

"Inside, Yank."

The deputy released his hold on Steve Merritt's arm and reached past him to open the door of the marshal's office. Merritt tensed, but the lawman's other hand never moved. Neither did the muzzle of the Colt revolver pressed against Merritt's spine. The hand came back to his shoulder, shoved him roughly forward.

"Inside, I said. I guess a night in jail will prove you ain't much punkins in this town."

Merritt took it silently. He'd tried to fight earlier, in the saloon, but this was different. His anger was under tight control now. He had no doubt that the deputy would shoot him, and he didn't mean to get killed tonight by some crazy ex-Reb. He'd waited too long for this day to lose it.

The marshal's office was lighted by a pair of coal-oil lamps. Their yellow glow reflected off the barrels of rifles and shotguns racked against one wall, behind the scuffed and battered desk that filled half the room. A man at the desk looked up in surprise as the deputy hauled Merritt before him.

"What's the trouble, Frank?" he asked quietly.

"This bluebelly was asking about Clint Davidson. When I tried to find out why, he got smart. Decided he wanted to fight."

He gave Merritt another shove, sending him staggering against the desk. Merritt started to turn, but caught himself in time, gripping the edge of the desk until his knuckles were white from the effort. He was a big man, medium-tall and solidly built. At thirty-three, he was giving up close to ten years to the deputy, but Merritt had the edge in size and conditioning.

The marshal looked him over thoughtfully, taking in the blood and bruises on his face, the torn clothing, the goose-egg swelling over his right eye.

"I'd guess he got the worst of it." The marshal shifted his gaze to Frank. "Did you do all that damage yourself?"

Merritt snorted. The deputy, Frank, took a step toward him and raised the Colt.

"Cells are in back, mister. Move, unless you'd rather be carried."

"Hold on."

The marshal's voice was still soft, but his words stopped Frank cold. Surprised, Merritt raised his head and looked at him for the first time. The lawman was burly and balding, with huge hands and wide, sloping shoulders. He looked like a backslapper and a joke-teller, except for his eyes. Straight on, they held something Merritt couldn't read, a sadness or a strange knowledge that changed his whole face. Those eyes were on the deputy now.

"I believe I'll visit with the prisoner for a while, Frank," he said. "Why don't you put that gun away and get on with your rounds?"

Frank hesitated, then holstered his pistol. With obvious reluctance, he drew Merritt's revolver from his belt and laid it on the desk.

"You'd better watch him, Marshal. He's quick. Maybe I should—"

"I expect I'll manage. You go along now."

Frank went out, not quite slamming the door behind him. For a moment, Merritt closed his eyes. He was tired and his head hurt. He'd had a long stage ride that day, all the way from the campsite on the Brazos where the Army was just breaking ground on a new fort.

When he'd last seen this part of Texas, it had been Comanche land, the ruins of Fort Phantom Hill to the south marking the outside limits of settlement. There had been no town here then, only a stage stand and a tent saloon. Now it was called Gilead, and had stores and a bank and a church. Riding in at dusk, he'd been pleased to see how the place had grown – pleased, at least, until he met some of the citizens.

Resting part of his weight against the desk, Merritt raised a hand to wipe his mouth, winced as he touched the raw, scraped flesh there. He pulled himself erect and glared at the marshal.

"That deputy of yours—" he began.

"My name's Bell." The marshal was examining Merritt's pistol with unhurried care. He spoke almost to himself, but for some reason, Merritt broke off his protest. "Don't believe I caught yours."

"Steve Merritt, Marshal. It's good of somebody to ask." He drew a deep breath and tried again. "Listen, that deputy of yours was lying. I didn't start any fight."

Bell smiled slightly. "Somebody sure did. I can tell you were in one." He put the pistol down, keeping his hand on it. "Have a chair. Frank called you a bluebelly. Is that right?"

Gratefully, Merritt sank into a heavy oak chair across from the marshal. "I was in the Union Army," he said stiffly. "I didn't know that was a crime."

"Reckon it's not," Bell admitted. "But it might explain some things. An officer, I'll bet."

"I went in as a lieutenant," Merritt snapped.

He hesitated, then set his jaw. Damned if he'd crawl to a bunch of Rebs, even if this was their town. "At the end, I was a major. I served with Sheridan in the Valley."

"Is that a fact?" Bell's face didn't change, but the sadness in his eyes came a little nearer the surface. "My boy was in the Valley, too, with General Early. He was killed at Cedar Creek in '64."

It caught Merritt cold, and at first he didn't answer. He'd been at Cedar Creek, too, but it hadn't been his fault the Rebs were there. It was their war.

"I'm sorry," he said at last, knowing how false it sounded.

Bell didn't seem to notice. "Me, too," he said. Then he straightened abruptly in his chair. "Frank mentioned you were asking about Clint Davidson. Why?"

Merritt's anger came back, and he half-rose. "It seems to me that's nobody's business but mine."

"Being a lawman, I get into a lot of things that aren't my business. But I still need to know." Bell waited a moment, then added, "Maybe there's some reason you don't want to talk about it."

"No." Merritt shook his head slowly. The marshal was partly right: He didn't want to talk about it, but not because he had something to hide. He just wasn't sure how to explain a dream. Spoken straight out, his reasons for coming back sounded weak and silly to him, but they had helped to carry him through four years of war.

"We're going into business together," he said. "The cattle business. Clint has the idea we can trail them north to the Kansas railheads."

"Seems reasonable," Bell said. He rubbed his chin. "I know about Clint. How do you come into this?"

"Clint and I soldiered together out here before the War. He was a lieutenant then, until he resigned his commission and went with the Rebs. He always said he was going to come back to Phantom Hill, where the old fort was, and settle down someday.

"About six months after Appomattox, I got a letter from him. We wrote back and forth some, and finally put together a deal. In his last letter, he said everything was ready, and—" He broke off to fish in his shirt pocket, then passed a folded letter across to Bell. "Here, read it yourself."

Bell smoothed the creased paper and turned it to the light. "Dear Steve," he read in a flat voice. "Glad to hear you're finally coming out. I've spent most of that Yankee money you sent me, and we need to get busy buying up stock. There's plenty around for anybody with cash. Laurie and Jory want to meet you, and we can trade lies about the War. You'd never have been happy, married to a Yankee gal and working in some office. Just ask anybody in town for the LJ Ranch, they'll tell you how to find our place."

Merritt interrupted with a bark of laughter. "Clint's advice was never much to count on." He touched the lump on his forehead and winced. "But that was about the worst piece he ever gave me. Anyway, he's known I was coming since October. I don't know why he never mentioned me."

"He did," Bell said. "October was five months ago. That's pretty slow hurrying."

"I had some things to finish up," Merritt said coldly. He'd told Bell about enough. The marshal didn't need to know about two older brothers who were glad to buy him out of the family business, or about Elizabeth.

Elizabeth. For a moment, he saw her face, her black hair tousled, her eyes glowing with love and warmth and hidden laughter. His life before the War, the years with the Old Army on the Texas plains, had never been more than stories to her. He'd never mentioned Clint, or Phantom Hill. Then, his dream of coming back was just that — a dream to help him through the fear and boredom of the War. Reality was Elizabeth and Ohio and a place in his father's shipping business when peace came.

They'd gotten engaged late in 1863 while he was home in Cincinnati recovering from a wound. Then he went back to the War. When he returned, she'd put off the wedding date once, and then again. Finally, she gave back his ring.

"You've changed, Steve," she'd said. "I don't know you anymore."

He tried to argue, but it was true. After their engagement, he'd reported back to the Army of the Potomac, just as a stocky, cigar-champing general named Grant took charge. In the next month, the Army had lost fifty thousand men in grinding, continuous battle. Merritt had changed, all right, at places like Spotsylvania and Cold Harbor and Petersburg. Something down inside him was different after that, and the dream had looked different, too.

Merritt shook his head, looked back at Bell. "I left Cincinnati three weeks ago," he said. "I took a riverboat to Baton Rouge — my family runs a packet line on the river — then rode the stage the rest of the way. If you don't believe me, check with Clint."

"Clint Davidson hasn't been seen for pretty

near three months," Bell said. "Just after Christmas, it was. He rode out one evening to check the stock and never came home. You can see why I might wonder about a stranger looking for him — or claiming to."

"But —" Merritt stared at him. "I wrote him when to expect me. He —" He straightened, his weariness forgotten. "Where is he, Marshal? What have you done to find him?"

"We've looked around and asked around. We tried to track his horse, but his woman didn't call us in until a couple of days later. Nothing's turned up."

"Look, if something's happened to him —"

"Now, why would you think that?" Bell interrupted sharply.

Merritt slammed a fist on the desk in exasperation. "What in hell do you expect me to think?" he demanded. "A man doesn't just disappear."

"Men have," Bell said. "It's a funny thing. There was a girl who lived out south of town, Jud Rankin's daughter — wild. She turned up gone about the same time." He spread his hands. "Talk is, they went off together."

Merritt rose and leaned over Bell, his fists planted on the desk top. "Listen, Marshal, Clint has a wife and kid. He called the ranch the LJ, after them. You'd better be careful how you talk about him."

Bell sighed. "Boy, I am careful how I talk about him. You think I'm just spreading gossip?" He rubbed his eyes with a big, square hand. "Clint still had some of the money you'd sent him, and he'd run around with the Rankin girl some last year, before he brought his family out here. It wouldn't be the first time—"

"He'd never steal. Not Clint. Not from me, or anybody else."

"How about the girl?" Bell asked. "You knew Clint pretty well, I'd judge, back before he was married. Would he do that?"

Merritt started a heated denial, then bit it back. Slowly, he sank back into the chair. Bell had a way of getting around his anger, of making him think.

He hadn't seen Clint for eight years, not since the day in 1859 he'd left Fort Chadbourne for a staff assignment. They had been young then — he only now realized how young. He'd gone on to Grant's army, and Clint had gone to the Rebs and every campaign from Shiloh to Bentonville. Merritt didn't know how the War might have changed Clint, but he knew how much it had changed him.

"Clint always liked a pretty face," he said at last. "Still, he never ran from anything. I can't say for sure, but offhand, I don't believe it."

Bell nodded. "Well, that ain't quite evidence,

16

but it's something," he said. "How about—?"

"Wait a minute," Merritt interrupted. "You saw Clint's letter. He knew when I was coming. Why would he wait until just before I got here to run out?"

"Good question. If he'd stolen your money, it's clear, but you don't think he did. Maybe to throw off suspicion."

"Whose suspicion? Nobody here knew I was coming."

"Except maybe Clint's wife," Bell said.

Merritt took a second to think about that. "I don't know her. That's your department. Is she the sort a man would run away from?"

"I wouldn't," Bell said. "She's quite a lady, but you never know what goes on between a man and a woman." He looked speculatively at Merritt. "I reckon you'll be meeting her."

Merritt hadn't thought that far ahead, but he saw Bell was right. "I suppose so. I've made a lot of plans, expecting to go partners with Clint. I'd better talk to her, at least, before I decide what to do."

"Well, her and the boy are out at Clint's place, just off the road and about three miles south of the old fort. Reckon you'll know the way." Bell pushed himself up out of his chair. "Nice place. Hard to believe a man would run off from it."

"Then why have you stopped looking for Clint?"

"Didn't say I had," Bell answered mildly. He took down a ring of keys from a hook behind him. "The bunk's pretty comfortable in that cell on the end. I'd recommend it. There's a washstand back there, too."

Merritt stared at him. "You mean I'm under arrest?"

"Well, not exactly. I doubt Ma Sullivan would rent you a room, and I don't much want you going back in that saloon tonight. So I'm offering you lodging and breakfast on the county."

"No thanks." Merritt laughed. "I can sleep on the ground. I think I'll find a horse and ride out a little way toward Phantom Hill, if it's all the same to you."

Bell stumped around to look down on Merritt. "It ain't," he said flatly. "Son, I don't think you understand. Those boys you bumped into tonight, Frank and the others, they ain't what you'd call reconstructed yet."

Merritt picked up his pistol from the desk, seated it in his military holster. "I'm not afraid of them," he said.

"That's what worries me. I don't think you've got good sense." Bell held up a hand to shut off Merritt's protest. "It's hard to find a family

18

around here that didn't lose somebody in the War. Cap Daingerfield, the saloonkeeper, he had a son killed at Nashville. Frank was in the Home Guard — the Texas Mounted Rifles. Only four of his company made it back. The others are about the same."

He waited for Merritt to answer, then shrugged.

"All right, there's another reason. I'm not easy in my mind about Clint. I'll look pretty blamed silly if you up and disappear the way he did. I just can't see letting you run off in the night, with half the town knowing you're here."

"I can look after myself."

"Reckon that's what Clint thought." Bell held out the keys, pointing with his other hand toward the cell block. "Now, that's enough. If nothing'll do you but being arrested, I can oblige. There's pillows and blankets in that chest back there."

Merritt stood up and accepted the keys, grinning crookedly. "Since you put it that way, Marshal, I don't see how I can refuse." He took a step, then stopped. "Oh, my luggage is still over at the stage stand. Can I be paroled long enough to get it?"

"I'll send Frank," Bell said. "Don't worry, it's safe enough with Ma Sullivan."

"Even though I'm a Yankee?" Merritt asked

19

with some bitterness.

Bell smiled at him. "Son, you'll find that folks here in Gilead are funny," he said. "Come tomorrow, one of them may take it into his head to shoot you, but they won't steal your bags."

"I'll remember that," Merritt said.

He turned away toward the cells with Bell's amused chuckle in his ears.

CHAPTER 2

Merritt rode south on the stage road next morning, splashing across the Clear Fork of the Brazos at a ford just below town. He was stiff and sore, and his bruised lips were puffy from the beating he'd taken the night before, but none of that took away from his pleasure at seeing the Phantom Hill country again.

His horse was a rangy bay, hard-mouthed and with a strong urge to run. He'd rented the animal at the livery stable, after a good breakfast in Bell's jail. Now, in the coolness of the spring morning, he was strongly tempted to let the horse stretch his legs.

The land here had hardly changed with the years. The river ran to his left, sluggish and salty, its banks overgrown with cottonwoods and tangled willow breaks. A few buildings straggled south from Gilead, and Merritt could see the smoke from a chimney or two ahead where before there had been only rolling buffalo range. Except for those few traces, he might

21

have been coming in from a week on patrol, with a column of cavalrymen behind him and Clint – First Lieutenant Clint Davidson – at his side.

"This'll make great ranchland, once we've settled it," Clint had said a score of times. "And I'm coming back and work it. If you understood about cattle, Steve –"

"I understand you'll get a Comanche lance through your gizzard if you don't pay attention to business. You're not safe just because we're across the river. A war party –"

"–ran off forty horses from the cavalry lines last month," Clint finished, grinning. He pulled off his hat and drew a hand through his bristling blond hair. "I know, General. What do they do at West Point to make you regulars so serious?"

"Anyway, we won't live long enough to see this place settled. We'll never tame it."

"Nonsense, my boy. Just picture me in a few years, settled down with a little wife –"

"That redhead from the laundresses' quarters, maybe?"

"–sitting on the porch in the evening with a drink in my hand, telling the little tykes how me and Uncle Steve used to fight the Indians."

Clint had joked about it, as he joked about everything, but he'd been serious enough to come back and look for his dream. The way

Bell told it, things had worked out pretty much as Clint had predicted. He had a wife and a son, a homestead near the site of the old fort, and old Uncle Steve come to join them. Everything had worked out — except that Clint was missing and the hick local lawman didn't seem to have much idea where to look for him.

A movement down by the river snapped Merritt back to awareness. He rose in the stirrups for a better look, then grimaced at his own caution. No Comanches were hiding there, no Confederate cavalry waiting to swoop down on him. Some big animal, half hidden by the trees, was grazing in the river bottoms. Somebody's cow, he thought, or maybe a browsing deer. Then it moved forward into a clear space and he saw that it was a horse, saddled, its reins dragging as if it might have pulled free from a hastily tied knot.

Sheer reflex made Merritt haul back on his reins and turn his own mount's head toward the thicket. It was automatic. You made yourself as small a target as possible, facing the place from which the enemy would come. He shook his head sourly. Maybe someday he'd stop acting like an old firehorse—

A shot came from the brush, a spurt of powder smoke marking its source, the bullet snapping past low to his left. Without conscious thought, he slid off his horse. His right hand wrenched his rifle from its boot as his left swatted the bay on the rump. The horse bolted, blocking the bushwhacker's line of fire for a moment, and in that moment Merritt dropped flat and found what cover he could.

Watching the drifting smoke, he levered a cartridge into the rifle's chamber. It was a Spencer carbine, the kind the cavalry had carried toward the end of the War. He'd bought it in Cincinnati especially to bring out with him. Now, he thought with grim satisfaction, it was going to give somebody an ugly surprise.

Merritt eased back the Spencer's hammer and fired toward the clump of brush. Immediately, the other rifle spoke again, this time from a point farther downstream. Merritt pumped the trigger guard, putting two bullets squarely into the middle of the new cloud of smoke. Without waiting to see the result, he sprang up, dashed fifteen yards on a slant, and dropped again.

There was no reply from the hidden rifleman. Merritt raised his head carefully to scan the tree line. The horse he'd seen earlier was out of sight among the thickets, and nothing moved in the area the last shot had come from.

He started to cock the carbine again, then changed his mind. He had four rounds left —

extra ammunition was in his saddlebags, still with his horse, wherever it was — and he meant to be sure where the next one went.

The Spencer held in front of him, he snaked through the grass toward the river. If he could get to a place where the gunman wasn't sheltered by the cutbank —

The third bullet was closer, plowing into the soft earth barely an arm's length from his face. He cocked the Spencer and snapped a shot back. Almost at once, there was a crashing among the brush, then the drum of hoofbeats on the solid ground across the river. Merritt had a glimpse of the horse laboring up the far bank. It broke into the open on a dead run, its rider crouching low in the saddle as he lashed the animal on. Merritt swore and ran forward, but before he could get a clear shot, the rider was well past the carbine's effective range.

"All right," Merritt muttered. He hadn't liked being a target in the War, and he found he didn't like it much better now. Somebody obviously didn't want him around. He didn't know if the ambush was only a hangover from last night, or if it was somehow tied in with Clint — but he meant to find out.

The bay had run off perhaps a quarter of a mile. It stood with its head down, trembling a little from the noise, but showing no inclination to lope back to the barn. It shied away when Merritt approached, but gradually he calmed the animal and caught the reins. He reloaded the Spencer with practiced haste, then mounted and rode back toward the source of the shots.

"For a man who's so quiet most of the time," Clint's voice said in his mind, "you sure take it serious when somebody shoots at you. Did they teach you that at West Point?"

"You're always riding me about West Point. What bothers you about regulars, anyway?"

"Sheer jealousy, I suppose. I was almost a graduate of VMI, but there was this girl — a lovely thing, Steve, with—"

"So that's how you ended up in the Army."

"I'd meant to all along, but not just that way. Still, she was worth it. Fortunately, my father and the Secretary of War are good friends, and he wrangled me a commission after a couple of years."

"Sure he did," Merritt said aloud. That Medal of Honor that Clint had earned in Wyoming Territory hadn't hurt his chances, either. Clint had a great future in the service, Secretary Davis — Jeff Davis, that was — had said.

Merritt found the tracks easily enough in the muddy riverbank, but no sign of the metallic hulls a Henry or Spencer would have left. In-

26

stead there was a trace of loose gunpowder and, nearby, a blackened ball of paper — the remains of a paper cartridge for a muzzle-loader. The footprints, scuffed and unrecognizable, told him only what he already knew: There was one man who didn't like him.

He swung back into the saddle, speaking quietly to the still-skittish bay. After that, he rode with the carbine across the saddlebow, his eyes tracking every shadow in the dense thickets along the river. Only when the trail swung up a low bluff and angled away from the river did he relax his guard a little.

Fort Phantom Hill stood on the grassy tableland at the top of the rise. Riding in as he'd done a hundred times, Merritt wasn't prepared for the way things had changed. He knew the barracks, nothing more than wood and cedar-shake cabins, had been burned by Comanches almost as soon as the post was abandoned. The few stone buildings were in better shape, but their walls showed signs of quarrying by settlers in search of building stone. Where the officers' quarters had been, gaunt chimneys stood sentinel among deep pits and man-high clumps of prickly pear. The parade ground was green from the first spring rains, and a covey of quail burst from the belly-deep grass almost under the bay's hooves.

Merritt reined in. He'd been away a long time. He could remember enough, though — long stretches of garrison duty, the patrols up through this country, how they'd used the old post for a campsite long after it had been officially abandoned. Over there, he'd carved his initials into the stone of the colonel's fireplace. Beneath those trees, the officers had gathered on the riverbank, smoking and talking, arguing tactics and women and politics and slavery. The Southerners had drawn apart toward the end, and the talk all revolved around one subject.

"It'll all go smash someday soon," Clint had said one night. "The country can't hold together, and the Army will break up with it."

Merritt answered lightly, though he knew it was true. "You'll never leave the Army, Clint. Not while there's money on payday and a loose woman within miles."

"I wish it was that easy." For a moment, Clint's expression was as serious as Merritt had ever seen it. "But nothing will make any difference between us, Steve." Then he grinned. "Molly's her name — that red-haired one. I think she's sweet on me."

The laundresses' shacks were long gone, their wooden walls returned to the earth. Merritt touched spurs to the bay's flanks and rode on.

He was passing the chimneys of officers' row when a rustle in the grass caught his attention. He turned, the carbine ready in his hands. He saw nothing, but almost at once the sound came again. This time, there was a hint of movement beside one of the stone foundations.

"Who's there?"

Without waiting for an answer, he dismounted, cocking the carbine in the same motion. He looped the reins around a mesquite limb and moved cautiously toward the ruined building.

The rock chimney was just to his left. As he stepped past it, the tail of his eye caught a small figure crouched in the old fireplace. He whirled, dropping to one knee to throw off an enemy's aim, bringing the carbine smoothly down into line. Then he saw the person more clearly and jerked the muzzle upward again.

The boy stood with his back against the roughly mortared stones, staring at Merritt with wide blue eyes. He looked to be six or seven years old, tall for his age, dressed in ragged overalls. His tanned, thin face was topped by an unruly mass of blond hair. He looked at Merritt, then at the carbine, and began edging away around the fireplace.

"Hello," Merritt said quietly. "I'm sorry about the gun, but you scared me. Do you live around here?"

The boy didn't answer. He was in the open now, clear of the ruins. He glanced behind him, then brought his eyes back to Merritt. One step at a time, he continued backing away.

"I'll bet you're Clint Davidson's boy," Merritt went on. "You look a lot like him. Is that right?"

The boy stopped, frowning at Merritt suspiciously. Abruptly, he nodded. Merritt grinned, thinking back to Clint's letters.

"That means you're — ah — Jory, Jory Davidson."

He stood up slowly. The boy poised to run, then held his ground.

"You're a good way from home, Jory. Where's your mother?"

"I'm right here, mister." The voice came from off to one side. It was low and soft, but there was a ring of command in it. "You just stand easy. Jory, come here."

Still looking at Merritt, the boy ran in that direction. Merritt waited, the carbine held easily in his hands.

"All right. Drop that rifle."

"I'll put it down, if you don't mind. This half-cock safety was never very safe." He bent and laid the gun gently on the ground. Straightening, he turned to face the woman. "You must be Laurie. Clint wrote me about you. It's a pleasure to meet you."

She wasn't at all as he'd pictured Clint's wife. She was tall, with a willowy slimness. Her hair was long and brown, caught behind her neck and falling free almost to her waist. Her face was pretty enough, but that wasn't what Merritt noticed first. Instead, he saw the firm line of chin and jaw, the clear eyes that met his squarely without a trace of fear. She was holding an old Walker Colt, gripping the heavy pistol with both hands. The hammer was back, and the muzzle was centered on Merritt's stomach.

"You haven't met me yet," she said. "You're just here, on our land, carrying a rifle. What do you want?"

"I came out to see you. I'm Steve Merritt. Clint wrote me—"

"I know what Clint did. Why did you need a gun to come calling?"

Merritt shrugged. "To tell the truth, I was nervous. Somebody took a shot at me a mile or so back. Last night, half the town jumped me in the saloon because they hadn't heard the War's over. Now you're pointing that cannon at me. I'm beginning to think I'm not entirely welcome around here."

The woman's eyes narrowed a trifle, but she

didn't answer directly. "How do I know you're telling the truth?" she asked instead.

"Well, I don't know," Merritt said in exasperation. "I could show you Clint's letters, but if you can't tell just from listening to me that I'm no Texan, that probably won't convince you, either."

She gazed at him a moment longer. Then Jory tugged at her skirt.

"Don't shoot him, Ma. He's nice. He just scared me for a minute, that's all."

She looked down at the boy, then back at Merritt. Finally, she lowered the pistol. Her eyes were still troubled.

"I'm sorry," she said. "It's just that — well — things have been happening — strange things. We came for a picnic, because Jory likes this place, but I think somebody's been here recently. There's fresh-turned dirt over by the old buildings there." She paused, shook her head. "I'm sorry," she repeated. "Ride back to the house with us."

"Thanks," Merritt said. He retrieved the carbine, then went to untie his horse. Laurie Davidson looked closely at the animal for the first time, and suddenly she began to laugh. It was a pleasant sound, and she seemed to mean it.

"I guess you really are a Yankee," she said.

"Mr. Culver gave you his butter-churn horse."

Jory giggled. Merritt looked sideways at the bay.

"Butter-churn horse? I know a little about horses, but that's new to me."

"If you put a can of milk on his back, he'd churn it into butter. That old horse can trot up and down beside a tree all day, and never get out of the shade. Mr. Culver saves him for—"

She put her hand to her mouth and stopped in sudden confusion.

"For Yankees and other dudes," Merritt finished for her. He rubbed his back reflectively. "Well, I've ridden worse, but not since I left the Army."

As they talked, she led the way back toward the south. A buckboard waited there in the shade of a spreading mesquite. It had been hidden from Merritt by a fold of ground when he first rode in, and he'd had no hint anyone was around. Well, so much for his keen senses. Maybe he'd forgotten more about the War than he'd thought.

He tied the bay to the wagon's tailboard and swung Jory up into the back. As he came to help Laurie up, she turned, smiling at him.

"You really are Steve Merritt," she said. "The one Clint talked about so much. I never thought you were real."

"Probably I'm not. Clint isn't one to let the truth stand in the way of a good story." He saw the change in her face, the sudden worry, and he spoke quickly. "The marshal told me what happened. I was hoping you could add something."

Laurie shook her head. "I don't think so, but I'll try." She closed her eyes for a moment. "I'm glad you're here, Mr. Merritt. I need to talk to someone."

"All right." Merritt handed her into the wagon seat, then stepped up beside her, leaning the carbine against his knee. He took the reins. "Let's talk," he said.

CHAPTER 3

Sometime just before the War, Merritt guessed, a determined homesteader had settled along the stage route three miles south of Phantom Hill. He'd quarried stones from the old fort to build a crude but solid house. Later, he'd starved out, and later still, the building's roof timbers had collapsed. The house was abandoned when Clint came out to file on the land, and he'd taken it over.

Now, sitting in the room that served as parlor and kitchen, Merritt could see how much had been done on the place, and how much remained to do. Two of the three rooms had a new roof — Clint must have had help with that, he thought — and a half-decked loft had been built over the parlor. The third room was still an empty shell, open to the sky.

"Clint intended to fix that up for Jory," Laurie said. She poured coffee for Merritt, weak coffee made from old grounds. "He was busy, though, getting the barn ready and cleaning out the well, and he just didn't get around to it. The cows came first, he always said."

Merritt looked around him. The parlor was crowded with furniture – cookstove, rough-built cabinet, a tall pie safe, a table and chairs cramped beside the front door. A worn horse-hair sofa stood against the far wall. Surprisingly, an upright piano occupied one corner. The bare wooden floor was scrubbed and spotless, and newspapers pasted neatly edge-to-edge covered the stone walls. The shuttered windows were covered with flour-sack curtains tacked around the edges.

"It looks fine to me." Merritt smiled at her. "That doesn't look like Clint's style, though. You must have done a lot of the work in here."

Laurie shrugged. "Not so much. We thought maybe in a year or so–"

She broke off abruptly, went to replace the coffeepot on the stove. For a moment, she stood motionless, her back to Merritt. Then she came back to the table and sat down.

"I'm sorry," she said. "You aren't interested in our plans. You asked today if I could tell you anything about the night Clint left."

Up in the loft, Jory stirred and made a small moaning sound. The boy hadn't been asleep long. He'd asked a horde of questions during supper about Ohio and Yankees and the old days with Clint. Merritt had finally carried him up to bed, promising more stories another time.

Laurie rose, her face turned upward. The sound wasn't repeated, and she sank back into the chair. "He doesn't see many new people here. He likes you."

"I like him," Merritt said. "He favors his pa." He stared at the tabletop for a time, searching for the right thing to say. "Laurie, about Clint—"

She nodded. "There isn't much to tell." Her voice was calm and businesslike. "He saddled his horse and went out toward the fort. He said he had to check on the stock. I thought it was strange — it was cold and raining, and almost dark. But he kissed me and bundled up in his old army greatcoat and told me not to worry and" — she paused, then went on steadily — "and that was the last time I saw him. At first, I thought he'd decided to stay at the fort — we were going to put a line camp there — to get out of the rain. Then when he still didn't come back, I rode out there, and then I went to the marshal."

"And the marshal didn't find anything."

"He tried. He and Frank Harmon spent the whole day searching for a trail. But the rain—"

"Sure. Bell told me." Merritt remembered

what else Bell had told him, the part about the Rankin girl. He pressed his lips together. "Look, you know I'm Clint's partner. We're going to find him, but we have business to think about, too. First, I need to find out what shape the ranch is in and get things running. Do you know what records Clint kept?"

"I kept the accounts. They're up to date." She stood up and crossed to the cabinet, reaching into a high shelf. "This is the ledger, and here's the record of the stock Clint bought with the money you sent. We had credit at the store, and the banker, Abel Whitlock, advanced me money to get through the winter."

Merritt looked up. "That was nice of him." It seemed odd, too, and he filed it away to think about.

"He's been a big help to us," Laurie went on. "So was Frank. He—"

"Frank? You mean Bell's deputy?"

"Yes, Frank Harmon. He wanted me to leave, but I couldn't as long as I didn't know what had happened to Clint. So he's come out every so often to see if we need anything."

"I see." Merritt rubbed his chin. "I'll take care of the banker tomorrow. Then, with your help—"

"I can't. We're not staying."

Merritt looked at her in surprise. She put the

ledgers on the table, then opened the door and stepped outside. After a moment, he followed.

She was standing on the porch, her arm around one of the corner posts. The night was clear. Stars hung low and close over the buildings, and a lopsided moon was setting behind the trees that lined the riverbank. Laurie was looking out to the west, toward the river and the open plains beyond. She didn't turn when Merritt came up.

"Laurie?"

"I waited for him at first," she said. "I thought – I hoped – that he'd gone off on his own, that he'd come back when he was ready."

She paused for so long that Merritt thought she wouldn't speak again. Then she said, "It could have been that way. There was a part of Clint I never knew, especially after he came home from the War – something I couldn't touch. Do you understand what I mean?"

Merritt didn't answer. He understood, all right. The woman didn't seem to notice his silence.

"Now I know better. Even if he didn't care about me, he'd never leave Jory."

She turned to face him. In the yellow light from the doorway, her face was calm.

"He's not coming home, Mr. Merritt. I know that now. There's no more reason for me to stay."

"But –" Merritt started to argue, but changed his mind. Instead, he asked, "Where will you go?"

"I have family back near near Waco – my brothers. I'll take Jory there. It's time for us to make a new start."

Merritt hesitated. On his own and with an unfriendly town to deal with, he was in for a hard time running the ranch, at least for a while. There was no place for her and Jory in his plans, and no way she could help to find what had happened to Clint. It was probably best that they leave, just as she'd said. Still, she was Clint's wife, and he remembered a passage from one of Clint's letters: Laurie and Jory are settled in already. The place is still rugged, but it's ours. Laurie says she'll never leave.

"Laurie?" Merritt asked. "Are you sure that's what you want?"

She gave a little laugh. "No," she said. "But what I had here is over." Looking out toward the plains again, she shivered. "It's getting cool. Let's go inside."

As she pulled the door closed behind them, she said, "You'll be taking over here, I guess. We'll pack tomorrow." She looked around the room. "I can send for the things we'll want, and you're welcome to the rest. Maybe it'll pay the bills we've run up."

"I told you, Clint and I are partners," Merritt said. "As far as I'm concerned, half the ranch is yours. But let's worry about that tomorrow. I'll ride back to Gilead and find a place to stay, and—"

"No!" The word must have come out with more force than she'd intended, because she reddened and looked down at the table. "I mean, it's late, and we have plenty of room. I could make down a pallet, or there's the sofa—" She stopped, then looked at Merritt. "I'd hoped you'd stay here."

Merritt was frowning, slowly putting things together. "You haven't told me everything, have you?" he asked. "You said something today at the fort about things happening. What did that mean?"

"It's probably nothing." Laurie busied herself with emptying cold coffee and pouring fresh cups. "At first, it was just noises in the night, and tracks, and the like. I thought I was just being weak, without Clint to look out for me. But last week, two of our cows were killed — shot — down by the river. It's like someone's trying to scare us off."

For the first time, Merritt realized the strain she'd been under for the past weeks. She'd been alone, with not even the comfort of knowing whether her man was dead or alive. She must have been afraid, for Jory if not for herself — but she surely hadn't shown it.

"Maybe it's the same someone who shot at me," he said. "You bet I'll stay. I wouldn't miss a chance to meet him." A thought struck him. "Have you told any of this to the marshal?" he asked.

She shook her head. "I told Frank, but he only said what everybody said — that we shouldn't stay out here alone. Now I see he was right."

"Maybe," Merritt agreed, but suddenly he wasn't quite sure. "Anyway, let's figure out where I'm going to sleep."

In the end, he slept in the barn. Laurie had argued against it, though she'd seemed relieved when he brought the idea up. He suspected she felt as awkward with the situation as he did. He had another reason, though, for wanting to get out of the house. If she was right, if someone was trying to drive them away, Merritt's arrival would surely worry him. He might try something tonight, and Merritt wanted any edge he could get.

The barn smelled of hay and old wood and the strong pungent odor of animals. It was soothing to Merritt after a long spell of civilization. He found a pile of straw in one corner and spread his blankets, then went to check on his rented bay and the other horses stabled there. By the light of a lantern, he carefully cleaned and reloaded the Spencer, leaning it against the stone wall within easy reach. Then he stripped off boots and shirt and gun belt, hanging the belt from a nail near his head. Blowing out the light, he settled down to think, to try to make some sense of the last couple of days. None of it seemed to fit together, though, and at last he drifted into sleep.

He awoke suddenly and completely, his hand going automatically to the smooth leather of his holster. It was still dark in the barn. Dimly, he saw the sleeping shape of the old plow horse in the nearest stall, the black tracery of harness against the lesser black of the stone wall. From the planks near his head, a cricket chirped busily.

Drawing the gun belt to him, Merritt lay listening. He remembered some hazy dream of the War and thought that might have awakened him. Then the sounds came again — the stir and clop of hooves, the creak of saddle leather, even the hushed murmur of voices.

Cavalry! his mind insisted, but he immediately corrected himself. He was awake, the War long ended. There was no need to worry about Rebel horsemen on midnight raids. Even so, riders, several of them, were passing just outside.

Merritt rolled to his knees. Working by feel, he unfastened the holster flap and drew out his Navy Colt. The air was sharp with the last chill of winter, but he hardly noticed. Softly, in stocking feet, he made his way to the big double doors at the front of the barn. They were still firmly closed, and he put his eye to the crack between them.

Riders, all right. The moon had been down for hours, but in the clear starlight they loomed up like giants. Six, eight, a round dozen, they drifted into the open yard between the house and barn. Balancing the Colt in his right hand, Merritt reached to unbar the door. Then he thought better of it. He didn't know who these people were, and it might be as well to find out before he started waving guns around. He could afford to let things develop a little more.

The horsemen formed up in a rough semicircle in front of the house, their backs to Merritt. When they were in place, one of their number rode a few paces forward.

"Merritt!" he yelled. "Come out here, Yank. We want to talk to you!"

It was a voice Merritt had heard before, Frank Harmon's voice. "Merritt," he bellowed again.

44

A light showed inside the house. After a couple of minutes, the door opened. Laurie Davidson stepped out on the porch. She'd lighted an old storm lantern, and she held it high to peer at the horsemen. Her hair, unbound now, tumbled below her shoulders. A white nightdress showed below the blanket she'd thrown about her. Behind her, Merritt saw Jory peeping around the edge of the door.

"Frank, is that you?" Her voice sounded puzzled and sleepy. "What's wrong? What is it?"

The deputy laughed harshly. "Merritt's the matter. Send him out here. We have business with him."

"Why, he's—" she began, then broke off. "What business? What do you mean?"

"We want to explain how we feel about Yankees mixing with our women."

"*Your* women!" At first, Laurie seemed shocked into silence. Then she took a furious step forward. "Frank Harmon—"

Merritt interrupted her. Lifting the bar quietly, he heaved against the left-hand door with all his strength. It slammed back with a splintering crash and he stepped into the open.

"Here I am, Frank. Start explaining."

The deputy started violently. He turned in the saddle, his hand dropping to the gun at his hip.

45

"Don't." Merritt's warning was punctuated by the click of the Colt's hammer coming back. "You'll never get it out of the holster."

Harmon stared at him, hardly seeming to notice the gun. "You! But, we thought — how — ?"

"What did you think, Frank?" Laurie's voice came out cold and cutting as the night wind, pulling the mob's attention back to her. She came forward, the lantern held high, until she stood directly in front of them.

"What did you expect to find?" She turned slowly from one to another, trying to find one who would meet her eyes. Some tried, but they turned away from the frozen anger there. "Josh? Sid Culver? What did you expect to find?" She stopped in front of the man on the end, and the hurt showed in her face. "And you, Mr. Drake. What did you expect of me?"

The man called Drake took off his hat, holding it by the brim with both hands. He was older than the others, and his hair was gray. He raised his head and looked at Laurie. His voice was soft, but clear and determined.

"We judged you wrong, Laurie — Mrs. Davidson. I should've known better, and the fault's mine. I'm awful sorry." He turned and inclined his head toward Merritt. "You, too, mister. I'm sorry for what we thought to do."

46

Merritt nodded sharply to him, keeping the gun steady on Frank. For a moment, no one else spoke. Then Laurie said, "I thought you were my friends." Her chin came up, and she stood erect before them. "Please go. Get off my land!"

The line of men stirred, their horses shifting restlessly. Somebody muttered, "Aw, hell." The third man from the end neck-reined his horse around and rode slowly out toward the road. One by one, the others followed. The deputy paused in front of Merritt.

"Listen, Yank. Don't think you can pull a gun on me and get away with it."

Merritt laughed at him. "Don't you think you'd better leave, Frank? Your army's retreating."

"I won't forget this."

"Neither will I. Now, get out of here."

Harmon spurred away into the darkness. Merritt listened until he was sure the hoofbeats were fading with distance. Then he released a long sigh and lowered the gun, easing its hammer down. Laurie had set the lantern on the ground and now stood with her face in her hands. Jory padded barefoot from the doorway to put his arms around her.

"Don't cry, Ma, it's all right. What did those men want, Uncle Tom and the rest?"

Merritt tucked the Colt into his waistband, wincing at the cold bite of the metal on his bare skin. He went to them and scooped Jory up.

"They just wanted to visit. They're gone now."

"Tom Drake," Laurie murmured. "I never thought he would—" She broke off and looked up at Merritt. "I guess I still thought — I mean, I called it my land."

"Sounded pretty good, too," Merritt said. He saw the tears coming then. Without thinking, he put his free arm around her trembling shoulders. She cried quietly for a minute or more, while Jory reached across to pat her hair. Then she pushed away from Merritt and raised both hands to wipe her eyes.

"I can't go away," she said. "This is our place, and I won't let anybody run me out."

"Good," Merritt said. She had broken for a moment, but only for a moment. He'd bet not many men had seen her cry. Looking into her tight-lipped face, he grinned, the kind of grin Clint might have worn.

"I'll help you," he said. "We're partners, remember?"

CHAPTER 4

It was late in the morning when Merritt returned to Gilead. He had driven the Davidsons' buckboard in, with the old farm horse between the shafts and the bay trotting nimbly along behind. Reining up at the livery stable, he dropped off the bay and its saddle, then went next door to Ma Sullivan's and claimed the rest of his baggage. There wasn't much of it, just a couple of carpet-bags, and he tossed them into the back of the wagon. Talking things over with Laurie the night before, he'd decided to move out to the ranch. It would be certain to cause gossip, but neither of them was especially worried about that just now.

Two men were loading supplies into a high-sided farm wagon in front of the general store. They straightened to watch as Merritt pulled the buckboard up nearby, but neither of them spoke. A tight checker game was in progress on the porch, the players and a couple of spectators too involved even to glance at him. Another

49

man – a buffalo hunter, judging by his clothing and his smell – sat by the open door, cradling an old Sharps carbine in his arms. Merritt nodded a greeting to him as he passed and got a cold stare in return.

"Morning, mister." The storekeeper stood up from a big wooden crate he'd been unpacking. Behind him, a plump, gray-haired woman was stocking shelves with airtight cans. The man wiped his hands and came toward Merritt, the beginnings of a smile on his face. "What can we do for you today?"

Merritt patted his pockets. "I have a list here, someplace," he said. "Here. And I'd like to pick up the Davidsons' mail."

The storekeeper's smile vanished. "Well, I don't know," he said, looking uncertainly behind him. "There's a good-sized account on the Davidsons already. Are you thinking of settling up?"

"I'm on my way to the bank right now," Merritt said. He noticed the woman had turned to watch. "If you'll put the order on that buckboard outside, I'll pay everything off when I get back."

"Well – sure, mister. We'll get right to it."

Merritt thanked him and left. He paused to look at the still-immobile checker players, then swung right and headed up the street toward the bank. It was a neat frame building, and unlike most of the town's other businesses, it had been painted at one time or another. For a bank, though, Merritt thought it looked pretty unsubstantial – anybody with a crowbar and a little time should've been able to break in.

Not until he got inside did he see the heavy iron bars on the door and windows. A single teller's cage stood at right angles to the door, with a blind wall behind it. Back in the far corner was a massive green safe, almost man-tall. The teller was young, and he looked uncomfortable in the sack coat that stretched tightly across his chest and shoulders.

"Something I can help you with, mister?" he asked.

Merritt started to explain his errand, but the teller interrupted almost at once.

"Oh, you're the Yank. Hold on a minute."

He sidled out of the cage, glancing at the safe to be sure it was closed, and went through a doorway into the back. As he moved, the skirts of his coat slipped back, and the butt of a big revolver showed at his hip. Merritt smiled to himself. It wasn't exactly like Cincinnati, but the banker here obviously had strong ideas about protecting his depositors.

In a couple of minutes, the teller emerged. "Mr. Whitlock wants to see you," he said.

51

"Right through here."

Merritt strode past him and found himself in an office lined with books and ledgers. A roll-top desk was set squarely in the middle of the floor. The man behind it rose and came around to offer his hand.

"Mr. Merritt? A pleasure to meet you, sir. I'm Abel Whitlock. I'm president of the bank here."

The banker looked smooth and self-satisfied. He was dressed in black broadcloth with a white linen shirt. His stiff paper collar was new and fresh, and a heavy silver watch chain drooped across the front of his vest. He smiled professionally at Merritt, his blue eyes cool and watchful.

"Sit down, sit down." He went back to his chair, pushing a box of cigars down toward Merritt. "I've been expecting you, of course. Clint – I'm sorry about his unfortunate disappearance, very sorry – told me a good deal about your partnership."

Merritt cautiously took a seat. "Did Clint also tell you I'd fought for the Union?" he asked.

"Why – of course, he mentioned that. I hardly see how it matters."

"It seems to matter to some people." Merritt touched the purplish swelling over his eye.

"Mind telling me why you're so glad to see me?"

The banker selected a cigar, examined it for a time. "I can see you like straight talk, Mr. Merritt. I'm a businessman. Holding a grudge isn't good business." He spread his hands. "I hope you'll go ahead with your plans for the LJ. In the long run, it'll be good for this town."

"And for the town's bank?"

Whitlock smiled again, but this time there was an edge in his voice. "I expect to profit from your operations, Mr. Merritt. I've always made a profit, whatever the circumstances. It's my hope we can help each other."

Merritt nodded slowly. He recognized Whitlock now, not the man but the type. He'd be a sharp, shrewd businessman, ready to stand with Merritt as long as that seemed the most profitable course. To be here in Gilead, his fortunes apparently undamaged by the South's loss of a war, he must have been an expert at playing both sides. Not a man who'd be expected to show much sentiment where money was concerned, Merritt thought.

Aloud, he said, "I think we can work together. Just one more thing, if you don't mind."

"As you wish," Whitlock said shortly.

"Why did you give Laurie Davidson a loan after Clint left?"

The question clearly caught Whitlock by

surprise. "I consider that a reflection on Mrs. Davidson's character, sir," he snapped, but Merritt thought the indignation didn't quite ring true. "I trust you're not suggesting my motives were dishonorable."

"No. I just want to know."

"Well, I'd been informed you were arriving soon to take charge of the ranch. I assumed that, as a gentleman, you'd be prepared to honor the debt." The banker still sounded huffy. "If you choose not to, of course the loss will be mine."

Merritt sighed. "Thank you," he said. He didn't think Whitlock was telling the whole truth, but it was all he was likely to get today. He reached into an inside pocket and withdrew a long envelope. "Here's a letter of credit for three thousand dollars. It's drawn on the Merchants' Central Bank of Cincinnati. I'd like to settle the debts against the ranch and open an account for the rest."

Whitlock raised his eyebrows. "That's a lot of cash for a town like this. We haven't seen much hard money here since the War." He opened the letter and read quickly through it. "Yes. I assume this means you intend to go ahead, even without Clint."

"That's right."

"You may have difficulty. The way people

here feel about Northerners—"

"I'll manage."

Merritt left it at that. After a pause, Whitlock cleared his throat.

"I don't mean to pry, but if I knew more about your plans, maybe I could be of service." He held the envelope up between two fingers. "It seems ridiculous to start by mistrusting each other."

Merritt considered, then nodded agreement. "You know we had some big ideas about taking a herd north. The way things are, that'll have to wait. What I need now is some good breeding stock and enough time to get my feet on the ground and some money coming in."

The banker gave his careful smile. "I believe I can help with the breeding stock," he said. "I'll make some inquiries. You'll have to buy the time yourself." He put the letter on his desk and picked up a pen. "Now, there are a few formalities, and we'll be in business."

As easy as that, Merritt thought as he left the bank a little later. Evidently, not everybody in town was after his scalp. He turned toward the store, then stopped abruptly. His friend the buffalo hunter was across the street, leaning against the hitching post in front of one of the saloons.

This time, Merritt had a good look at the

man. He was dressed in greasy buckskins, with a black slouch hat crushed low on his forehead. Black hair shot with gray straggled below the hat brim, and a heavy black beard hid most of his chin and jaw. The general effect was more like a bear than a man. He wasn't someone who'd be easy to forget, and Merritt was sure he'd never seen him before today.

Another new acquaintance, Merritt thought sourly. He'd probably been at Gettysburg, and had been waiting ever since to get a crack at a lone Yankee — or maybe the buffalo hunter was just curious, and Merritt was so spooked he was jumping at shadows.

He paused in front of the general store. The buckboard was still there, standing empty. He'd meant to go on to the marshal's office, but instead he stepped into the store again. The storekeeper and his wife were back at work on the shelves. Another man, apparently a customer, was idly considering three big jars of candy at the end of the counter. The storekeeper saw Merritt and came hesitantly toward him.

"Ah — mister, I'm sorry, but I don't think we can fill your order." He produced Merritt's list and held it out. "I've got my regular customers to think of, and our stock's short right now."

Merritt didn't move to take the list. He shifted his gaze past the storekeeper. The back third of the big room was piled almost to the ceiling beams with bags of flour and cornmeal and dried beans, with kegs and crates that were still unopened.

"I see," he said softly. "I thought the Davidsons were regulars here. Laurie thought so, too."

The storekeeper looked down at the counter, his face screwed into a frown. After a moment, the other man broke the silence.

"I guess that was before they took up with Yankees, mister. Henry, give me a nickel's worth of this horehound."

"Sure, Mr. Garvey."

Quickly, the storekeeper put down the list and moved down the counter. Merritt followed, watching as he scooped the candy into a bag.

"It's not going to work," Merritt said conversationally. He spoke to the storekeeper, but his eyes were on the man called Garvey. "It'll take a little longer to get things freighted in from San Antonio, but I can do it. You aren't going to starve us out."

"Mister," the storekeeper began plaintively, but Garvey interrupted him.

"Then we'll find some other way." He was about forty, lean and sharp-featured, and he eyed Merritt expectantly. "We don't want your kind around here. You want to make something of that?"

Merritt saw that he'd shifted the bag of candy to his left hand. His right was hooked into his belt, inches from the low-cut holster he wore. Merritt felt the anger rise in him, but there was something else, a cold warning that stirred the hairs on the back of his neck. Someone was in the doorway behind him, he knew. This was no challenge — it was a trap.

Carefully, he turned back to the storekeeper. "You said there was a bill. How much do I owe you?"

"Listen, mister, you understand how it is—"

"I understand. How much?"

"Hey, Yank," Garvey said. "I ain't finished with you."

"You don't fight in here!"

Merritt had forgotten the gray-haired woman until she spoke. She slammed one of the cans down on a shelf and came briskly over toward the group at the end of the counter. "Now, Grace," the storekeeper chided, but she ignored him. Stopping in front of Merritt, she looked up into his face.

"Twenty-seven dollars, mister. That's the tally."

Merritt took out two gold coins, laid them

on the counter. "Thank you, ma'am. Sorry we can't do more business."

She studied him a moment longer, then made up her mind. "Henry's mistaken." She reached for the list, read it over. "We can take care of you. It'll be just a spell."

"You're getting into something that's not your business, Miz Evans," Garvey warned. "You'd better—"

"Don't you tell me what I'd better do, Adam Garvey," she snapped, turning on him. "Whatever happens in this store is my business, and don't you forget it. Now you get out of here." She gestured at the doorway. "And take that other trash with you. Henry, don't stand there. Get this gentleman's order filled."

Garvey stared first at her, then at Merritt, his quick-moving eyes assessing chances. Finally, he turned away. "Another time, Yank."

Now Merritt could look at the doorway, but it was empty. He gave a whistling sigh and smiled at the woman.

"Thanks. I don't think he likes me."

She snorted. "I don't think much of you myself. But you pay in hard money, and I never did hold with cold-decking a man. You go along. Your goods will be ready in about half an hour."

Merritt tipped his hat to her and went, pausing at the door to glance both ways. The buffalo hunter was back across the street, but now Garvey was talking earnestly to him. Keeping one eye on them, Merritt strode toward the marshal's office.

Marshal Bell was at his desk, his posture suggesting he hadn't moved since the last time Merritt had seen him. He nodded morosely when Merritt came in.

"Morning. The bad penny turns up. I hear you had a little trouble out at the Davidson place."

Merritt gave a bark of laughter. "You didn't hear that from Frank, I'll bet."

"People tell me things," Bell said. He still looked half asleep, but Merritt doubted that he was. "They said he stopped by to see if you needed a little hanging. He won't do it again — I talked to him." He paused, and his expression turned serious. "Frank's been a good deputy. He's hotheaded, but folks around here like him. If you've got a complaint—"

"No, that's not why I'm here. I just wanted to tell you I'm staying on. I'll run the ranch the best way I can — until one of us finds Clint."

Bell didn't react to the prodding. "I figured as much when you went to see old Whitlock. That Jory's a fine boy, and Miz Davidson is a right handsome woman."

60

"Now, listen," Merritt began angrily. Then he saw the sleepy smile in the marshal's eyes and caught himself. "All right. But I'd like to know what you've done about finding Clint."

Bell sighed. "That's just what this town needed," he said. "Another irate citizen. Well, I went out and tried to track him the day Laurie reported him gone, but it was like tracking a duck across a pond. Then I sent Frank around the county asking questions, but nobody had seen him. Finally, I put out a circular on him and his horse, asking anybody who could help to write me. I sent it to county sheriffs and marshals around here, and one to San Antonio for luck – cost the county twelve dollars."

He spread his hands. "That's about all. We don't know there's been any crime, and it's gol-durned hard to find somebody that don't want to be found."

Merritt turned away in helpless anger. Bell was right, but Merritt was sure that Clint hadn't just left. There must be some way to find out.

"You mentioned a girl last time – Rankin?"

"Mary Beth Rankin. Her folks live out east of here, close to Tom Drake's place. She's seventeen or so. Likes men, especially if they've got a little money. Run away a couple of times before, last time with a local boy, but they drug her back."

"Her parents — what are they like?"

Bell frowned. "The woman's all right. Old Jud—" He considered. "Well, if Frank's set on hanging somebody, he'd be a good choice. Clint never had anything to do with them, but he knew the girl well enough."

"Maybe if you talked to them—"

"I did. The old woman hasn't no idea where she is, and Jud don't rightly care."

His back to the marshal, Merritt stared through the window with unseeing eyes. There must be something he was missing. If Clint had really been involved with the Rankin girl, things would look different — but Merritt still couldn't quite believe it was that simple.

He shook his head impatiently. Then, suddenly, he focused on the scene outside. The big man and Garvey were still there. "Marshal?" Merritt said. "Could you step over here a minute?"

Bell levered himself to his feet and came around the desk, his brows raised questioningly. Merritt nodded toward the pair.

"Those two are mighty interested in me, Marshal. Can you tell me who they are?"

"Big one's named Witherspoon, he says," Bell answered promptly. "They call him Baldy, 'cause there ain't much hair under that hat. Carries a Navy Colt like yours and a big Bowie

62

knife. Comes through here every few weeks and causes trouble."

"He has an old Sharps carbine. Some of them still take paper cartridges, don't they?"

The marshal studied Merritt briefly. "Most likely. I've seen a lot fixed up for metallic shells, but buffalo hunting's not a job where you need to shoot fast." He waited, then asked, "Any reason you should wonder about his?"

Merritt shrugged. "Somebody took a shot at me yesterday. I thought it was a muzzle-loader, but it could've been his Sharps — or anything else. How about the other one — Garvey, is it?"

"Adam Garvey." Bell took another look, then returned to his chair. "He works for Tom Drake, sort of. He's about as mean as Baldy, and a lot smarter. You met him?"

"I did," Merritt said. "I don't know what he could have against me, though."

Bell chuckled. "Son, you just being here is enough for most folks." He tipped his chair back and thought a moment. "But if somebody did do harm to Clint, they might be after you, too. You want some advice?"

"Anytime, Marshal."

Bell pointed at Merritt's army-style gun belt. "If you're set on carrying that six-gun, cut down your holster so's you can reach the gun the same day you need it. That's one part. The second thing is, don't use it. You can't win a gunfight here."

Merritt grinned. "We'll see," he said.

"That's not what I mean." Bell sounded annoyed. "Son, if you shoot somebody, the town'll hold a nice fair trial and string you up. You can't win."

Merritt thought of the setup in the store, of Garvey's attempt to force a fight. Maybe Bell wasn't the only one thinking that way.

"You might be right, Marshal," he said. "But whoever starts the trouble won't be around to testify. I'll be seeing you."

He stepped out and looked at the two men standing by the saloon. Garvey turned away quickly and went inside, but Baldy Witherspoon merely spat in the dust, his hungry, unblinking gaze meeting Merritt's. Unconsciously, Merritt dropped his left hand to his holster and unfastened the flap. Back at the store, he checked the buckboard to see that the supplies were there, then went inside.

"One more thing," he said when the storekeeper came to wait on him. "I guess I need a new gun belt."

CHAPTER 5

Sitting on the bunkhouse roof, his legs dangling over the side, Merritt watched Jory hammer a last nail into the weather-beaten shingles. The boy tapped a couple of times to set the nailhead into the wood, then raised his head expectantly.

"Is that the right way, Steve? Won't the water get in?"

"I hope not. We won't know until the first good rain." Merritt squinted at the sky. The day was moving into evening now. He'd been working, with Jory's eager help, since lunchtime. "We're finishing up just in time for supper. Gather up those tools and bring them over here."

"Sure, Steve."

Merritt felt for the top rung of the ladder, stepped over onto it. He carried the tools to the ground, then reached high to catch Jory by the waist and swing him down. Finally, he went back for the Spencer carbine. He'd grown accustomed to having the Spencer always with-

65

in reach, as he'd grown accustomed to the un-
familiar feel of the open-topped holster behind
his right hip. Since his visit to Gilead a week
before, the weapons had been constant com-
panions.

Hefting the carbine now, Merritt thought
back to that day. Laurie had been waiting for
him when he'd returned to the ranch. He
hadn't seen her at first, but she'd come into
the barn while he was unharnessing the horses.

"Steve, did you see Mr. Whitlock?"

"I saw him."

Merritt's mind was still on Adam Garvey and
the ambush – if it had been an ambush – in
the store. He hardly thought of her question.

"What – what did he say? What about the
ranch?"

This time, he heard her voice, the overtones
of strain and worry. He turned to face her. Her
lips were set in a smile, but there was no sign
of laughter in her eyes. Her hands twisted at a
bit of sewing she must have been working on
when she'd heard him come in.

"Everything's fine," Merritt said. "He's all
for the idea – thinks there'll be a lot of money
in it for him." He started to tell her about
Garvey and Baldy Witherspoon, but instead he
said, "Whitlock's a good businessman."

Laurie looked away for a moment. "I wasn't

going to get all tearful about this." She shook her head in annoyance. "The place means a lot, though, to me and Jory." She looked up at Merritt. "It's going to be all right, now, Steve. Really all right."

Thinking of Garvey and Frank Harmon and the others, Merritt didn't share her certainty. But Laurie was really smiling now, her eyes still showing the hint of tears that had angered her, and Merritt grinned in reply.

"Sure it is. And the first thing I'm going to do is fix up the bunkhouse. A man could freeze to death in that barn."

The repairs took longer than he'd expected. Some of the old roof timbers were rotted and Merritt had no lumber to replace them, so he'd torn out most of the rafters and started over with a simpler framing. He used Clint's tools, twice going into town for things he couldn't find around the place. Laurie had begun to worry that the job was taking time needed for surveying the stock and making plans to build up the herd, but Merritt reassured her.

"From what you've said, these cows have been on their own since Christmas. A few more days won't hurt them much."

Actually, he knew she was right, but he welcomed an excuse to stay near the house until he was sure there'd be no more visits from

Frank and his friends. Besides, it had been a long time since he'd been able to work with his hands — before the War sometime, when things were still simple. Even having Jory hanging around hadn't spoiled that. In fact, to Merritt's surprise, both he and the boy had enjoyed it thoroughly.

"Are we really finished?" Jory asked. "Maybe I ought to put some more nails in the shingles."

Merritt broke off his thoughts. Leaning the Spencer against the wall, he dropped down beside Jory in the shade of the bunkhouse wall.

"I don't think so," he said, careful not to smile. "But we'll have enough to do later, when your ma and I get this place running. We'll need corrals, and stock pens, and a lot of other things. I meant to ask if you'd help."

"Boy, sure!" Jory said. "Can we start soon? I didn't know you were so good at building things."

"I learned from my father. He was a carpenter before he got into the river trade." Merritt waved a hand vaguely toward the north. "He built keelboats at first, for people coming south from Ohio."

"Is he rich?"

"He got rich before he died. He wasn't when he started out."

The money had never really mattered to his

father, either, Merritt thought. The boats mattered, the trim white side-wheelers that ran the Mississippi and Ohio in the days before the War. His father had loved them like children, and he passed some of that feeling along. Merritt had shipped as an under-clerk at fourteen and gone clear to New Orleans. He'd signed on every summer after that, as long as he was in school, but he'd never had any head for the way the business was run — his brothers had that.

Merritt shook his head. It was past now, the big steamers gone, replaced by short-run packets. The War had brought in railroads and killed the long-haul trade. Well, the War had killed a lot of things.

"My pa says we'll all get rich from the cattle," Jory says. "After we sell them up north, he says we'll get a big house and a new spring buggy and a pair of grays for me to drive. But he always laughs, so I don't know if he means it or not."

"We'll ask him when we find him," Merritt said.

A step sounded from the direction of the house, and Merritt automatically twisted to reach for the carbine. Then he relaxed sheepishly as he recognized Laurie's voice.

"Hello? Where have you all gotten to?"

Merritt answered, and she came around to the side where they were sitting. Today, her long hair was tied into a single braid, and an old straw hat protected her face from the sun's glare. She tilted back her head and peered at them from under the brim.

"I thought I heard the hammering stop. Are you ready to get washed for supper?"

Merritt rose. "Sure," he said. "Jory and I were just planning our next move. We're finished here."

Laurie started to answer, but Jory broke in excitedly, "Steve said I was a lot of help, Ma, didn't you, Steve?" He jumped to his feet, reaching for the hammer. "Can I go straighten nails? We may need them later."

"Tomorrow, young man," Laurie told him. "And you call your elders mister, not Steve."

"Aw."

"Now, run on and wash. We'll be right along."

"Yes, ma'am." Jory gave Merritt a man-to-man look and a shrug. "I'll do the nails later, Steve — Mr. Merritt, I mean. Can I?"

Merritt laughed and waved a hand. Jory scampered off toward the house.

"He's a good boy," Merritt said.

Laurie nodded. "He's really changed since you came," she said. "It's almost as though

70

Clint never—" She stopped abruptly, her lips pressed together. "No. I'm sorry. I had no business saying that."

Merritt looked at her. She stood against the rough stone of the wall, her arms folded. Beneath the wide brim of the hat, her eyes held neither coyness nor invitation, only a gentle sadness.

"You're quite a woman," he said on impulse.

She studied him, seeming to search his face and his words for hidden meanings. "Not so much, I'm afraid," she said seriously. "Remember, I was ready to quit. I — we would've been lost if you hadn't come when you did."

"I don't think you'd ever be lost."

Merritt turned away abruptly, began to gather up the tools. He was saying too much, and that wasn't like him. There was something about this woman that got past all his usual defenses. He would have to watch that. He had a ranch to run, and that was all.

"I'll move my gear from the barn. The bunkhouse isn't very homey yet, but I can manage. Then we need to get to work on the herd. Maybe—"

"Not now," Laurie interrupted, laughing. If his sudden change in tone surprised her, she didn't show it. "You're as bad as Jory. Hurry along, and we'll talk over supper."

71

Merritt drew a bucket of water from the tall brass-barreled pump by the barn, then stripped off his sweaty shirt and rinsed down his face and arms. The water had a bitter, alkaline taste, and its touch burned on his lips. Water had always been a problem in the Phantom Hill country, even back when the fort was active. The river was too prone to flood in winter and dry up in summer, and the shallow wells had limited capacity at best.

He would have to do something about water during the dry months, Merritt thought, if they were going to run many cattle. The river could supply the western part of the LJ, but the eastern pasture needed another source. A deep well with a windmill, maybe, or earthen tanks to hold the rainfall. Maybe Clint had already made plans for that. He would ask Laurie — or she might have some ideas of her own.

"Hello the house!"

The shout interrupted Merritt's thoughts. He quickly toweled his face dry with his shirt, then strode out to look toward the road. A man was walking along the wagon ruts toward the house, leading his horse. Merritt recognized him at once. He'd been in the mob with Frank that night — the older man that Laurie had called Tom Drake. Resting his hand on the butt of his Colt, Merritt waited for him.

"Evening," Drake called. He looped his mount's reins over a corral post and came forward slowly with the hesitant gait of a man more at home on horseback. He'd left his gun belt slung across his saddle, Merritt noticed. In the clear evening light, he looked nearer fifty than forty. His leathery brown face was creased into a tentative smile.

"Evening, Mr. Merritt. I'm Tom Drake." His faded blue eyes flicked to Merritt's right hand, still at his holster. He didn't offer a hand. "I – well, I saw you the other night–"

"I remember," Merritt said. "What's on your mind?"

Drake rubbed the back of his neck in embarrassment. "Well, Mr. Whitlock, down at the bank, said you were interested in some breeding stock. I got a little place a ways east of here. I thought maybe we could do some business." He hesitated, and then his eyes met Merritt's squarely. "If you're interested in dealing with me, that is."

"I see." Merritt remembered Drake, all right. He'd apologized, first to Laurie and then to him, and he'd had a hand in breaking up the mob. And Jory had called him Uncle Tom. "So far, it's been the other way around – I'm the one nobody's interested in dealing with. You have some cattle for sale?"

"I could part with maybe fifty head – heifers. I've got a couple of good bulls, but I'm not really looking to sell them. Maybe you'd like to ride over for a look."

"Maybe so," Merritt said cautiously. He didn't really think this was another trap, but he couldn't be sure. "It's a neighborly offer, anyway."

Drake studied the ground at his feet. "Nothing neighborly about it," he said. "My place ran down bad in the War. I've built the herd back up some, but right now, I'm stock-poor. What I need is cash to meet my bills and pay the taxes, if I'm going to keep the place." He looked up quickly. "I'm not asking for any handouts, but if you're in the market—"

"I'm in the market," Merritt said. He thought for a minute. "I've got a few more things to work out before I can think about moving in more cattle. Suppose we talk again in a couple of weeks? Maybe then I'll be ready to deal."

"Well, fine. Just let me know when you're coming, and I'll make sure to be there." Drake hesitated, digging at the ground with the toe of one boot. "Look, Merritt, about the other night—"

"Forget it," Merritt said roughly.

"No, listen. I ain't making excuses for myself – I should've known better. But don't think too hard of those other boys. They just believed Frank, that's all. They didn't mean any harm."

"They had a funny way of showing it," Merritt growled. "Never mind. I'll send word when I'm ready to look at your stock."

Drake started to answer, but the door of the house opened and Laurie came out onto the porch.

"Steve? Steve, supper's getting–" Seeing Drake, she stopped abruptly. "Oh – I'm sorry. I hadn't seen anyone come up."

Drake turned quickly toward her, snatching off his hat. "Guess I've been keeping him, ma'am," he said. "Him and I were talking a little business. I was just leaving."

"You needn't hurry, Mr. Drake." Laurie's momentary confusion had left her. "I'm just putting supper on the table. Will you join us?"

"No. No, thank you just the same. Reckon I'd better be getting home."

He stumped back to his horse. As he untied the reins and mounted, Laurie came across the yard to stand beside Merritt.

"Come back and visit soon, Mr. Drake," she said. "You're welcome here, anytime."

Drake's weathered face reddened. He nodded to her awkwardly. "Much obliged, ma'am –

Laurie," he said. "Good evening to you."

Drake reined his horse around toward the road. Watching the rancher go, Merritt was suddenly conscious of Laurie's nearness. She had baked bread for supper, and some of the scent reached him from her hair and clothing. Then Drake was lost in the gathering darkness and Laurie looked up at Merritt.

"He said you talked business. What did he want?"

The question sobered Merritt. He turned back toward the house, imperceptibly widening the distance between them. Laurie listened in thoughtful silence while he went over the conversation with Drake.

"It must have been hard for him to come here," she said finally. "He's a proud man." She frowned. "Why did you put him off? It sounds like he's offering just what we need."

"Maybe. We don't want to seem too interested, though. If he wants to sell now, he'll want it worse later on."

Laurie glanced sideways at him, a little frown wrinkling her forehead. Merritt thought for a moment she was going to answer, but instead she said, "We'd better go in. Supper will be cold."

She swiftly dished up the meal — chicken with dumplings and last fall's green beans —

while Merritt searched out Jory. He'd expected her to raise the subject of Drake again, but she didn't. For some reason, that annoyed Merritt.

"We won't be ready to buy cattle until we know exactly what you have here," he said at last, picking up the conversation where they'd left it. "Do you know how many head are running under the LJ brand?"

Laurie shook her head. "We started with about two hundred," she said. "Clint said that was a beginning, just through the winter. Then after he—" She hesitated, glancing at Jory. "After Christmas, we lost some, one way and another."

"All right." Merritt pushed his plate aside. "Tomorrow, I'll take one of the horses and ride out the valleys. Most of what we have left should be grazing there by now."

Jory bolted a mouthful of chicken and tugged eagerly at Merritt's sleeve. "Can I come?" he demanded. "Please. I'll be a lot of help, and I can show you where everything is, and—"

"Whoa," Merritt said gently. "It's going to be a long day's ride, Jory. I'd better go alone the first time." He met Laurie's eyes over the boy's head. "We need to hire a couple of hands, too. We'll need help later on."

"Maybe we can get someone from town," she

said doubtfully. "A lot of the men are out of work. But I'm not sure now—"

She stopped, and Merritt realized what she was thinking.

"—but now there's a Yankee here, they won't work for you?" he finished angrily. "What's wrong with these people? I've never seen anything like it."

"You've never lost a war." Laurie's voice was soft, but there was something unyielding behind it. "Don't forget, I'm one of these people. So is Clint."

"Well, I'm not!" Jory put in suddenly. "When I get big, I'm gonna be a Yank."

The unexpectedness of it caught Merritt off guard. His anger dissolved into a whoop of laughter. Laurie choked on a swallow of milk. When she could get her breath again, she glared first at Merritt and then at the boy. Finally, she, too, began to laugh.

"You'd better be glad your father didn't hear that, young man. He'd skin you good if he was here."

"Aw." Jory was embarrassed and a little irked by the laughter. "Well, he ain't here. Maybe he ain't coming back." Struck by a sudden thought, he turned to Merritt. "Steve, if he doesn't come back, can you stay and be my pa?"

The smile on Laurie's face froze, then came

apart in shock and remembered pain. Hearing her sharp intake of breath, Merritt spoke quickly and lightly.

"Oh, I'll stay around, but your pa's not likely to let me take his place. I'd better be — oh — your uncle, say." He scooped Jory out of his chair, propelling him toward the loft. "Now, you'd better get ready for bed, before your ma skins us both."

Later, in his cot in the bunkhouse, he remembered Laurie's face. She'd been hurt again, shocked by the realization Jory could forget — actually was forgetting — his father. He'd seen something more, though, a dawning wonder in her eyes. Maybe she was finding she could also forget.

Angrily, Merritt rolled over to stare into the rafters. What if she could forget? There were probably plenty of ex-Rebs waiting to take Clint's place. Merritt was the outsider here — everyone he'd met, even Laurie, had made that clear. He'd better remember it.

He lay awake for a long time, remembering it, before he went to sleep.

CHAPTER 6

Merritt was up early, but he found Laurie and Jory already at breakfast. Laurie wore a long divided riding skirt.

"Somebody has to show you the place," she told him briskly. "You'd end up wandering around all day, otherwise. I'll pack us a lunch."

"What about Jory?"

Laurie rumpled the boy's hair, and he made a face at her in return. "He'll look after the house and do his chores. I think today you'd better use the horse he usually rides."

"Aw." Jory stuck out his lower lip. Then he suddenly relented. "You don't need to be afraid of Jeff Davis," he said to Merritt. "He's nice. Pa says he rides just like a rocking chair."

Jeff Davis proved to be a tall gray gelding of advanced age and amiable disposition. He stood with lordly indifference while Merritt saddled him and slipped the carbine into its boot. Laurie, mounted on a compact brown mare, led the way eastward toward a wooded knoll. At the edge of the trees, she reined up and turned to wave to Jory.

"Are you sure it's safe to leave him?" Merritt asked. "I can manage by myself. I've done it before in this country."

"No, he'll be all right," Laurie said. "Clint and I had to leave him a lot when we first came here. He'll stay near the house, and we'll be back before dark." She gave a little laugh. "Kids grow up fast here. This fall, he'll be riding to school in town."

Merritt thought she'd intended to add something else. If so, she changed her mind. Kicking the mare into a trot, she turned up the slope.

"Come on. You can see most of the ranch from up here."

The crest of the knoll was rocky and bare of trees. The land fell away in both directions. The roofs of the ranch buildings lay to the west, with the line of trees that marked the river not far beyond. Merritt's eye followed the winding green ribbon north until he lost it in the distance.

Laurie pointed. "The fort's just about there. We've filed on everything from the river east until you reach the Drake place." Then she dropped her arm. "But I keep forgetting — you probably know this country better than I do. I guess you patrolled here in the old days."

Down the eastern side of the hill, the land dipped into a wide shallow valley, its floor carpeted with new grass. Scattered groups of longhorn cattle, maybe thirty head in all, browsed along the gentle slopes. Merritt remembered seeing buffalo grazing that same valley. The fort had been active then, and the river was the boundary between white man's land and the Comanches. It was a place to approach carefully, with scouts out to warn of an ambush.

Ambush. The shots fired at him earlier had come from the trees along the river, too. He'd almost forgotten, but it seemed that for him, times hadn't changed so much.

"It was hard country then."

"Now it's our best range." Laurie looked at him, a little frown wrinkling her forehead. "You must have liked it, even then. You planned to come back."

"That was a long time ago," he said. He nodded toward the longhorns. "Are those ours?"

"They must be. We moved most of the herd up by the old fort last fall – Clint had cured some hay there for winter feed. These probably strayed from there." She shook her head and sighed. "I'm afraid we've lost a lot by now. They've been on their own since Christmas."

"They'll have to stay on their own a little

82

longer, too. We need hired help to run this place right. Let's look this bunch over — if I can get Jory's rocking chair to move."

He urged Jeff Davis forward, and the horse broke into a reluctant trot. Laurie brought the mare along behind. Close up, the cattle didn't look promising. Lean from the long winter, their coats still rough and shaggy, they broke away slowly before the horses. Then one old mossy-horned steer pulled up short and turned to face Merritt.

"Look out!" Laurie called. Merritt looked back at her in surprise. At almost the same moment, Jeff Davis planted his forefeet and stopped.

Caught off balance, Merritt swore as the saddle horn gouged into him. He couldn't see anything that might have spooked the gray — only the steer, and Jeff Davis was supposed to be a cow horse. Merritt used his spurs, but the old horse only shifted from side to side. He was obviously as close to the longhorn as he was going.

The noise and movement startled the steer. He bellowed once, shaking his wide sweep of horns toward Merritt. From somewhere behind him, Laurie started to shout a warning.

"Steve, be—"

At the sound of her voice, the steer put his

nose down and exploded into motion, hooves kicking up clods of dirt in his charge, the wicked horns coming down to level on Merritt and the gray.

Before Merritt could react, Jeff Davis gathered his legs under him and sprang aside. The quickness of the move almost left Merritt hanging in the air, but he snagged the saddle horn and hung on. The steer turned like a cat, only to find the gray facing him again. He threatened another charge, and Jeff Davis slowly backed away. With a last satisfied shake of his horns, he turned and trotted away after the others.

"Steve, you ninny!" Laurie reined in beside him, her voice sharp. "Range cattle are wild — crazy mean, sometimes — after a winter. Don't you know to be careful?"

"I do now." Merritt rubbed the gray's neck ruefully. "I'm glad you gave me a smart horse."

"I thought you knew cattle. You said you'd spent three years here before the War."

"There weren't any cows here then," Merritt said. "Just Comanches." He leaned forward in the saddle and looked at her, a little nettled by her tone. "Listen, my job was finding money and markets. Clint's the one who knew cattle."

Laurie didn't answer. She sat motionless on the mare, her hands clenched on the reins, her face turned a little away from Merritt. Afraid

he'd upset her, he reined closer. "Laurie—"
Then she looked up, and he saw she was trying desperately not to laugh.

"Oh, Steve, I shouldn't have yelled at you,"
she said. "But I was scared, and you looked —
you looked so silly hanging onto Jeff Davis
while that steer—"

She put her head down and her shoulders
shook. Merritt recognized the reaction, had felt
it himself — the wild urge to laugh once the
danger was past. He recognized it, but that
didn't make it any easier to take when the
laughter was aimed at him.

"I'm sorry," Laurie said, when she could
manage to talk. "You were right, though. We'll
have to hire some help, somebody who knows
as much about cattle as Jeff Davis."

Merritt yanked the reins, bringing the gray
around. "From what I've seen of people here,
I'll take my chances with the cattle," he snapped.
He saw the quick hurt cut through the laughter
on Laurie's face, but it was too late to unsay
the words. "Let's find the rest of the herd."

Laurie pulled a little way ahead, and Merritt
didn't try to catch up. He was still angry, more
with himself now than her. Even more, though,
his run-in with the steer had reminded him of
a lot of things he'd been ignoring. The reality

he was facing looked a lot different than he'd expected.

By filing on open land and buying up other claims, Clint had tied up enough acreage for several thousand head of cattle. The problem was building up that kind of herd. From what Merritt had seen so far, he was sure the best of their cows had been stolen or scattered after Clint vanished. There was no chance of joining up with a drive in the coming summer. He would have to build for next year, and that would take money – more than he'd expected. The money he'd deposited with Whitlock's bank was supposed to last until the ranch started paying its way. Now, it looked as if that wouldn't be enough.

Merritt had counted heavily on Clint, as a cattleman and as a friend. He hadn't gotten that close to anyone for a long time – since sometime in the War. Too many men he'd known and liked had died in the grinding fights before Richmond. Then, it had paid not to have too many friends.

When he'd first found Clint gone, he'd figured he could carry on without him. Now, the whole idea seemed a lot more doubtful. It had only taken one old steer to show Merritt how little he knew about cattle. Without outside help, he had a woman and a young boy to teach him –

86

and it seemed he couldn't even get along with them.

"It's getting on toward noon."

Laurie's voice pulled him out of his thoughts. She had stopped a little way ahead. Shading her eyes, she pointed to a scrubby grove of oaks on a low hill.

"It'll be cool under the trees," she said. "We could stop for lunch."

Merritt didn't feel much like eating, but he nodded agreement anyway. He followed her up the hill, then picketed the horses to graze while she spread a cloth under one of the larger trees.

"We have some fried chicken," Laurie said, laying out things from the mare's saddlebags. She seemed quieter than she'd been at the start, and she didn't look directly at Merritt as he settled across from her. "And I put these pickles up last fall."

He took a drumstick and bit into it. "Thanks. This is good," he said. It was funny, but he was hungrier than he'd thought, now that the food was in front of him. He looked at Laurie, but she was gazing off at the hills to the east.

"The grass looks good here," she said without turning her head. "There's better near the fort, but something kept spooking the cattle. Clint had meant to build a line shack and keep someone out there."

"Sounds like a good idea, if we had somebody to do it."

"We'll manage," she said. "This range could take a cow every five acres. We can't manage that many, but we can start."

Merritt considered her. She was determined enough for both of them, he thought. She'd stayed all during the winter, and there were a lot of things against a lone woman. When he'd first met her, it was true she'd seemed ready to quit, but now he doubted that. She just didn't seem to be the quitting type.

"You mean to make this work, don't you?" he asked.

"You bet I do!" Then, as if surprised by her own intensity, Laurie turned to him with a little laugh. "I've never had anything that was mine before," she explained softly. "My pa sharecropped, and we never owned anything — not even the house we lived in. In the Army, it was the same. That's no way for Jory to grow up."

"No," Merritt said.

"Anyway," she went on briskly, "most of the ranchers around here need money — like Mr. Drake — and there's no market around close. We should be able to get breeding stock at a good price."

Merritt paused over a bite of chicken, then

finished it. He'd been away from Texas long enough to forget a few things, he thought wryly. He tried to picture Elizabeth, sitting under a tree back in Ohio and casually discussing cattle breeding.

"Steve, did I say something funny?"

"No, I was just thinking," he said. Even in Ohio, he suspected, Laurie would never be exactly ordinary. "You've really made a study of this business, haven't you?"

"I had a lot of time, while Clint was — was away," she began. Merritt broke in.

"In the War, you mean. You can say it. He's not one of the Rebs I'm having trouble with."

For a second, Laurie's eyes looked deep into his. "I wonder," she said. "If he were here—"

Wherever that idea was taking her, she broke it off. "Anyway, I knew he planned to settle here. We'd talked about it a lot." Almost defiantly, she added, "And I didn't mean to be a helpless woman on the place. I know a bull from a steer."

This time, Merritt couldn't quite control his reaction. Laurie must have seen it in his face, because she smiled with a hint of the old mischief in her eyes.

"Why, Steve. I think I've embarrassed you."

Merritt couldn't think of a good answer to that. Instead, he said, "Listen, about the cattle — you said the local ranchers don't have a market?"

"Why, no." She looked puzzled at his sudden change of subject, but went along. "Later on, when your idea of driving herds to Kansas catches on, things will be different, but—"

"The Army's moving back into Texas," Merritt interrupted. Against his will, he felt a little excitement slipping into his voice. "They're building forts all the way out the El Paso road, and soldiers eat beef. Why isn't anyone selling it to them?"

A minute passed in silence. Down the hill, a roadrunner strutted from the brush, caught sight of the horses, and raced away in an awkward, flapping run. Merritt watched it. He knew the answer, he thought. Because they're Yankees.

"The Army isn't interested," Laurie said at last. "You have to get a contract, and they pay by vouchers. It might take months to get the money. The bank and the storekeepers won't wait."

"They should. The system's slow, but it does pay off. If a man's credit was good—"

"Nobody's credit is good. Not unless they have the right connections — or Northern money." For the first time, Merritt heard bitterness in her voice. Then her expression changed, and she met his eyes anxiously. "Steve, I didn't mean that — not about you. It's just—"

"I know what it is."

And he did know. He was coming to see how foolish he'd been to think the War was over. Here, it wasn't finished at all. This time, though, he was going to make the Rebs' attitude work for him.

Laurie might have read his thoughts. "It's not the way you think," she said. "The people here need time, that's all. They aren't against you."

"Yeah. I've seen that."

"Well, they aren't, whatever you think. You can get along with them." Rising quickly, she gathered the tablecloth into a ball. "You could even enjoy today, if you'd stop pulling into your shell like an old terrapin every few minutes." She tried to look angry, then shook her head and laughed. "Come on. I'll show you the rest of your ranch."

The valley took them north and then east. In the lowlands, the first wild flowers were shouldering through the tall grass. Clouds of orange butterflies danced among the blossoms, rising to scatter on the wind when the horses came near. Laurie gave up to the sheer pleasure of the day, racing the mare far ahead and calling back derisively to Merritt. She was always finding some reason to laugh at him, he thought with a trace of resentment. Then he smiled wryly. He wasn't sure he'd want her to change, even if she would.

The ride took longer than they had expected. As the sun began to sink in the west, Laurie's high spirits gradually began to fade.

"We should be getting back," she said finally. "It's getting late, and we promised Jory."

"My fault," Merritt said, but Laurie shook her head.

"No. It's been so long since I could turn the worrying over to someone else, I'd forgotten what it was like." She paused, looking into Merritt's face. "I didn't want it to end," she said. After a moment, when Merritt didn't answer, her cheeks reddened and she turned away. "We'd better hurry."

"All right." Merritt knew he should say more, but the words were locked up somewhere down inside him. He raised himself in the stirrups, scanning the country around them. "We can head due west and cut the stage road above Phantom Hill. That's probably the shortest way home."

Laurie nodded quickly. "Let's go."

The sun went down over the wide sweep of

plains beyond the river. A rain shower was falling far out on the prairie, and the last light built the clouds into towers of red and gold. Merritt and Laurie rode in silence while the colors faded into the clear gray-blue of evening and the land sank into twilight.

When they reached the stage road, they spurred their horses into a trot. Jeff Davis started out smartly, but gradually reverted to his shambling walk, so that Laurie was perhaps a hundred yards in front when they reached the foot of the hill where the old fort stood. Halfway up, she reined in and waited for Merritt.

"Maybe it would be quicker if I walked," he began, smiling, as he caught up. Then he saw her urgent signal for silence. He kneed the gray closer. "What's wrong?"

"Up at the fort. I saw a light — just for a second."

"It's probably nothing," Merritt said, but he was already drawing the Spencer from its boot. At his side, Laurie stiffened in the saddle.

"There!"

This time, he saw it too — a flicker of light, up where the chimneys stood black against the sky. It reminded him of heat lightning on a summer night, or of the dark lanterns the Rebs had used for scouting.

"Off the road, quick."

They dismounted in the shelter of a clump of cat's-claw. Merritt caught Laurie's arm and pressed the gray's reins into her hand.

"I'm going to look. Stay here."

"What? No. I'm coming, too."

"Stay here!" Merritt repeated, as sharply as he could in a whisper. "What if these horses pull loose? Do you want to walk back to Jory?"

She twisted her hand free angrily, but didn't argue further. Cautiously, he moved off up the hill.

He swung wide to his left, away from the road and the horses. He didn't really believe anyone was up there, but that was no reason to take stupid risks. If bullets did start flying, he didn't want them going in Laurie's direction.

With that thought in mind, he levered a shell into the Spencer's chamber. There was still light in the sky, and that gave him an advantage. Anything moving along that crest should show up a lot more clearly than he would. If nothing went wrong, he could get the first look at anyone who might be up there.

Almost immediately, something went wrong. Merritt had slowed to work his way through a clump of low brush when the light came again. It was clearly a lantern, glowing from behind one of the ruined chimneys. Dark shadows of two or three men moved against the light, and

94

Merritt could almost make out the murmur of voices. He gripped the carbine, concentrating on moving in complete silence. As his foot came down, a rabbit crashed from the brush not an arm's length away and bounded desperately off into the night.

The light vanished. Merritt dropped to the ground, instinctively rolling to one side. He came up hard against a boulder and waited, the Spencer held close to his chest and the smell of crushed leaves in his nostrils. From the hilltop, hoofbeats sounded — more than one horse, ridden hard, going south along the road.

By the time Merritt could get to his feet and reach the spot where the lantern had been, the sounds had faded. Laurie was calling from the other direction. He answered, and she came up on foot, leading the horses.

"Are you all right? I heard noises."

"Mostly me," Merritt said in disgust. "I kicked up a rabbit and spooked everybody within earshot. Whoever was here left in a hurry when they heard me."

"That way?" Laurie's voice was suddenly breathless. "Steve, Jory's down there alone."

Merritt grabbed the gray's reins. "Not for long," he said. "Let's ride."

CHAPTER 7

In the afternoon sunlight, the old fort was peaceful and deserted. Crows called to one another from the cottonwoods along the river, and a pair of buzzards glided overhead on motionless wings. Merritt drew up the spring wagon near the spot where he'd seen the light the night before. Though he figured it was useless, he passed the reins to Laurie and swung to the ground, reaching back to get the Spencer. Jory jumped down from his seat in the wagon bed.

"Can I come, Steve? I'll be careful, honest."

"Better not. You look after your mother. I'll just be a minute."

Up by the chimneys, Merritt found a stain of oil, obviously from a lantern. The dry red soil around the foundations held scuffed footprints, none of them clear enough to identify, and the tracks of three horses led away toward the road. Merritt followed them until they were lost in the confusion of later marks left that morning by horses and farm wagons. He wasn't too surprised. He'd meant to investigate much earlier in the day, but he'd had a lot to do first.

Thinking of that, he touched the bulky sheaf of letters in his pocket to be certain he hadn't dropped them. Then he shrugged and strode back to the wagon.

"About what I expected," he said as he reclaimed the reins. "Somebody was here, but they didn't leave much of a sign. I wish we hadn't been in such a hurry last night."

"I know. I was worried about Jory, though."

"Huh!" The boy leaned forward between them, hooking his elbows over the back of the spring seat. "Don't see why you worried about me. I was all right."

Silently, Merritt agreed. Whoever had been at the fort must have gone right on past the ranch house. He and Laurie had come home to find Jory peacefully asleep in the loft, with the ladder drawn up and Clint's old shotgun beside him. Jory, Merritt had decided, could probably look after himself.

"Probably it was just a pair of sweethearts," Laurie said. "They came out here to be alone, and we scared them out of their skins."

Merritt snorted. "Pretty careful sweethearts. Either they had a lookout or awfully good ears."

He guided the wagon to one side of the road

and reined up as the westbound stage swept up the long grade from the ford. The six-horse hitch strained up the hill and stretched into a long trot as the big coach cleared the crest. Standing in the wagon bed, Jory waved to the driver, who responded by swinging his long whip in a circle and bringing it up with an explosive crack over the backs of his team. Pitching and swaying, the stage clattered out of sight behind the ruins of the fort, and Merritt snapped the reins to start the wagon forward again.

"I might talk to the marshal after I mail our letters," he said. "I'll ask around some, anyway. And we need to see if we can hire some help."

Laurie frowned at him. "You be careful. It won't make things better in town if you get into another brawl."

"If I—" Merritt bit the sentence off. He recognized the concern behind her words, but he didn't want any lectures today. "It wasn't exactly my idea last time," he said. "Ask your friend Frank, if you see him."

"Frank Harmon! He'd better not speak to me, after that trick the other night! If he thinks—" Hearing herself, she stopped. "Well," she said after a moment, "I never told you I wouldn't brawl. And don't look so smug just because you talked me into writing those Yankee forts."

"Those Yankee forts pay good money for beef," Merritt reminded her. "As far as Banker Whitlock is concerned, government promissory notes are gold-plated. And we should have a good shot at getting a beef contract" – he looked sideways at her – "with my Yankee connections."

Laurie pressed her lips together and didn't deign to answer. While they'd talked, the wagon had splashed through the shallow ford and up into Gilead's main street. Merritt drew the team to a halt in front of the livery stable.

The wide double doors were open and the interior of the building was dark. From someplace inside came the ringing of a hammer on iron. The hammering stopped while Merritt was helping Laurie down from the wagon. A few moments later, a man in a leather apron came through the doors into the sunlight. He nodded shortly to Laurie.

"Howdy, Miz Davidson." His eyes shifted to Merritt. "Something you want?"

"I'd like you to stable the horses. We'll probably be here the rest of the day. And–"

"Stabling's a quarter apiece," the man said gruffly. "Grain extra." He caught the headstall with practiced ease. "I got them. No, pay me later."

99

He turned his back and led the team inside. Looking after him, Merritt recognized the bull neck and the set of the shoulders. The blacksmith had been one of Frank's mob at the ranch. He was surprised he hadn't noticed it before. Just a matter of seeing things from the right angle, he thought.

"Laurie, why don't you take Jory up to the store and wait for me," he said quietly. "There's something I need to do here."

She hesitated, looking at him. "What is it? Is something wrong?"

"Not a thing. I just wanted to talk to — what's the stableman's name? — with Mr. Culver. I'll be right along."

"Well — all right." She reached out a hand to Jory. "Come on, Jory. I'll bet Mr. Evans has a piece of candy for you at the store."

Merritt waited until she and the boy were a few steps on their way, Jory tugging impatiently at Laurie's hand. Then he turned toward the yawning dark doorway of the livery stable. The day before, he'd put aside his doubts about Clint and the ranch and Gilead. That decision still looked good to him. If he meant to stay in Gilead, though, there were a few things he needed to start clearing up right away. His face set, he stepped inside.

Within the stable, the light was dim. The

interior smelled of hay and manure and the warm, musky scent of animals. The wagon stood in an open area beneath the high peaked roof, but at first Merritt saw no sign of Culver or the team. Then the gate to one of the stalls swung open, and the blacksmith came out. Dipping a bucket full at the water trough, he started back toward the stall. As he turned, he saw Merritt silhouetted against the light of the doorway. He stopped abruptly, waiting as Merritt walked toward him.

"You're Sid Culver?" Merritt asked.

"That's right." Culver was almost as tall as Merritt, and his bare arms were corded with muscle. He looked at the bucket in his hand, then set it down carefully, squaring around to face Merritt. "What of it?"

"You know me," Merritt said. "I'm half owner of the LJ, Clint Davidson's place. I want to buy a good saddle horse, one that knows cows."

Culver frowned, seeming to go back over the words in his mind. "Sounds like you mean to stay around," he said slowly. "Some of us figured you'd go back North."

"You were wrong. I'm staying."

"Yeah?" Culver raised his head and looked at Merritt, the challenge plain in his eyes. "I don't know as you're welcome here."

101

"I'm not asking you. I just need to buy a horse."

The blacksmith stared at him a moment longer. Then the man reached some decision inside himself, and his face cleared.

"Horses are my business," he said. "Check with me in about a week. I'll see what I can find."

"Thanks," Merritt said. In his mind, he let out a long sigh of relief. It looked as if Culver was a reasonable man. "I'm planning to hire a couple of hands, too. If you know anybody who wants a job, pass the word."

Culver shook his head. "All right, but I doubt it. There's some as needs the work, right enough, but I don't think—" He broke off, then shrugged and went on to the end: "I don't think they'd sign with a Yank."

Merritt turned away. "I figured that. Thanks, anyway."

He stepped out into the sunlight. There it was again. A sudden anger rose in him, and he clenched his fists. He almost wished Culver had taken him up — the urge to hit out at somebody, anybody, was almost too strong to resist.

"Hey, Yank." Culver was in the doorway. "You might try Cap Daingerfield's saloon. Anybody out of work, chances are Cap's got them on his tab."

"Yeah." Merritt rubbed his jaw thoughtfully, remembering the fight his first night in Gilead. "I guess I'll try there. I know the place."

Jory was perched on the porch railing outside the store, sucking at a peppermint stick and watching the nonstop checker game. He slid down and followed Merritt inside. Laurie was at the counter with Grace Evans, studying a mail-order catalog.

"Those curtains are a real bargain," the older woman was saying. "Just bleached muslin, but they'll be real pretty. I could order them for you."

"Well—" Laurie looked up and saw Merritt. "Oh. Just a minute, please." Straightening, she came over to him. "We're just looking at some women's things. Are you all finished?"

Merritt nodded. "Just about. Mr. Culver's going to find me a horse." He took the sheaf of letters from his pocket. "I wanted to drop these here to be mailed, and then I'm going over to the saloon and see if we can hire some help."

"Can I come?" Jory asked eagerly.

"To a saloon?" Laurie demanded. "Certainly not. We'll stay here and visit with Mrs. Evans." Glancing back to see that the woman was busy with another customer, she lowered her voice. "She's glad to see me, even if she does think I'm living in sin with a Yankee."

Merritt felt his face coloring. Looking at Laurie's mischievous smile, he was sure that was just what she'd intended. Before he could manage an answer, Jory piped up.

"Steve? What does 'living in sin' mean?"

"Your mother will explain," Merritt told him. "I'll be back soon."

From the shade of the porch, he looked out on the busy street. Saturday was the day folks came to town, and the saloon was sure to be crowded. Merritt almost wished he had picked another day. Then he shrugged and seated the Navy Colt more comfortably in its holster. This time, at least, he didn't intend to let himself be dumped on the marshal's doorstep.

Before Merritt reached the street, Frank Harmon came out of the marshal's office. His badge gleaming, he strode purposefully along the boardwalk. As he came level with the store, his eyes caught Merritt's and he stopped dead. His expression shifted from surprise through tight-lipped anger and on into something Merritt couldn't read. With a quick glance back toward the office, he turned away and pushed through the door of the saloon.

Merritt considered a moment, then settled on the porch to watch the checker players. If he wanted trouble, here was his chance — he figured he and Frank would have trouble enough any time they met. In spite of his earlier impulse, though, trouble wasn't really what he wanted. For this trip, he would do his best not to start anything. If the Rebs wanted to start it, that was their lookout.

Only a few minutes passed before Frank emerged. Hardly looking at Merritt, he walked rapidly up the street toward the bank. Merritt waited until the deputy was inside, then crossed to the saloon. The big room was full of talk and laughter. Eight or nine men were lined up along the rough wooden bar, and twice as many more sat at scattered tables. Back in one corner, a tall, angular man was dealing faro, and a group of poker players clustered at a table near the back. Adam Garvey sat alone in a chair against the wall, his bright eyes fixed on Merritt. The thin-faced cowhand's expression was almost pleasant, and Merritt felt a warning ripple run along his spine. He shifted so the holstered Colt moved against his hip, and Garvey looked away. Merritt watched him a moment longer, then stepped into an open space at the bar.

"Help you, mister?" Cap Daingerfield asked. Then he recognized Merritt and the smile dropped from his face. "Oh, for — I thought we were rid of you last time. Didn't you get the idea?"

The volume of talk dropped off as men turned to look, so that Merritt and Daingerfield faced each other in a gradually widening pool of quiet. The lanky gambler riffled through his deck of cards, and all at once the sound was startlingly loud in the room.

"I need two good men to work cattle at the LJ," Merritt said into the silence. "Thirty a month and found. Sid Culver thought you might know of somebody."

"I'd see you in hell first." The saloonkeeper's voice held a quiet intensity. "Get out of my place."

Merritt looked at him for the space of a dozen heartbeats. Daingerfield's son had been killed in the War, Marshal Bell had said. It showed in his eyes, in the pinched hatred on his face. Merritt swung away from him to look out at the others in the saloon.

"You all heard," he said. "If any of you are interested, I'll be at Evans's store."

His answer was a low murmur and a general shifting of feet and chairs. Nobody would come, Merritt realized grimly. All right, he'd tried, but he didn't need these Rebs. Scotty Macdonald, his old sergeant, had often talked of coming West after the War. Scotty knew cattle — not longhorns, but he could learn. A foreman's job and maybe a small interest in the place would bring him, and there were others. If the people here wouldn't accept Merritt, he'd do without them.

He had started toward the door of the saloon. Behind him, he heard Adam Garvey say, "Now, Billy." And a heavy hand fell on his shoulder.

"Hey, Yank."

The voice was harsh and challenging. Merritt realized he'd been expecting something like it from the moment he'd come into the saloon. With an almost joyful upsurge of his anger, he shook off the hand and wheeled to face its owner.

The man was a hulking, flat-faced bruiser. An old gray forage cap was perched on the back of his bullet head, and he tugged at its cracked brim as he planted himself before Merritt. He wasn't wearing a gun, but he didn't look as if he needed one.

"Hey, Yank," he repeated. "You don't look so tough. What regiment was you in?"

Merritt set his feet, hands loose and ready at his sides. "Fourteenth Ohio, Johnny. If you met them, you'll remember."

The big man laughed mockingly. "Hell, I was in Third Texas. We stacked you like cordwood at Cold Harbor."

Merritt hadn't expected that, nor his own reaction to it. For an instant, it took him out of the dim, crowded world of the saloon, so that he saw and felt and smelled again the ravaged countryside of the Virginia barrens — the damp heat, the flies, the long, ordered ranks of blue-clad corpses strewn in front of the Confederate earthworks. Then it was gone, and he was looking into the Reb's craggy face.

"You sure did," he admitted softly. "We left a lot of good men at Cold Harbor."

"Ain't no good Yankees," somebody yelled, and there was laughter. The big man stared at Merritt, his brow furrowed in childlike concentration. His eyes were blue and strangely innocent.

"I mind how they kept coming," he said. "They kept coming, when any fool could see they couldn't break our lines." Sudden suspicion clouded his face. "How'd you get through it, Yank? Was you one of them coffee coolers of a quartermaster?"

"My company was in reserve. The fight was over before we got orders committing us. We didn't charge."

A low impatient murmur ran through the waiting crowd. "Get on with it, Billy." Merritt recognized Garvey's voice. "He's still a blamed Yank."

The man called Billy might not have heard. "Orders!" He spat out the word. Then his eyes wavered, and he looked down at his feet. "We come through that real good," he said, his voice so soft Merritt could hardly hear him. "But then later. At Fort Stedman. Then Sayler's Creek. That's when—" The words trailed off. "Orders!" he said again.

Merritt realized he'd forgotten to breathe. Relaxing balled fists, he reached out to put a hand on the other's shoulder.

"Reb," he said, "I'll buy you a drink on that."

The big man blinked a couple of times. Then, like sunlight dawning across a rocky cliff, a wide grin spread over his face.

"Yeah," he said. "That's right. Hey, Cap, bring two beers."

"Listen, now, Billy," Daingerfield began. His voice held a note of uncertainty now. "I ain't serving no Yankee—"

The words trailed off into a croak. One of Billy's huge hands had closed on the saloon-keeper's collar. Almost gently, he drew Daingerfield closer.

"The Yank's all right, Cap, him and me. You bring us two beers."

He straightened his arm, sending the man crashing back against the shelves behind the bar. Daingerfield glared resentfully, but he drew two mugs and slammed them down on the bar. Rubbing at his throat, he sidled away.

Talk picked up again in the saloon, some of it harsh and angry. Merritt's companion didn't seem to notice.

"Funny," he said. "I hadn't thought of them days for the longest." He wiped a hand on his pants, then stuck it out to Merritt. "I'm Billy Troop. Simple Billy, they call me, but I ain't hardly so simple as you might think."

Merritt smiled. "You already know my name – but I'll answer to Yank."

A chair clattered back, and Adam Garvey stomped over to Daingerfield, planting his fists on the bar.

"If you're gonna let Northern trash in here, I ain't staying."

Daingerfield raised his hands in a helpless gesture toward Billy Troop. Still angry, the cowhand swung around on Troop.

"And you'd better watch who you're running with, Billy. Don't forget who your real friends are."

Billy swung his head around like a hound casting for a scent. "You mean you?" he asked, sounding puzzled. "You was the one set me to bust his head."

"Shut up, damn you!"

Garvey's eyes flicked to Merritt, showing sudden alarm. A couple of the other men at the bar scrambled out of the way, leaving

110

Garvey glaring at Troop.

"You keep quiet, you stupid—"

Troop's left hand swept out in a lazy arc. The movement looked slow and clumsy, but before Garvey could move, it caught him a backhand swipe on the side of the head and sent him spinning backward along the bar.

"Don't talk like that," Troop said mildly. "We was regulars. You was one of them heel flies in the Home Guard." He waved a hand at Merritt, his voice rising with excitement. "We got our discharges, the Yank and me, to show we fought good. Let's see your discharge!"

Garvey staggered erect, shaking his head dazedly. His face was white with rage.

"I'll show you my discharge," he screamed, and his hand streaked for his pistol.

Cramped in by Troop and the bar, Merritt never even thought of his own gun. Shouting a warning to Troop, he dived for Garvey. His shoulder socketed solidly into the lean cowhand just below the wishbone, driving him back. Garvey's breath whistled out, but he caught himself against the bar and rammed a knee up into Merritt's belly. Merritt sagged against him, took a heavy, chopping blow across the shoulders, and rolled free. He came to his knees not knowing if Garvey still had the gun. Belatedly, he went for his own holster, realizing even as he did so that he was too late.

Garvey was set, his six-gun coming up to center not on Troop but on Merritt. His vulpine face held a look of triumph that Merritt had an instant to wonder about. Taking his time, Garvey rocked the hammer back. His finger began to close on the trigger.

Merritt launched himself in a desperate lunge for Garvey's legs. He fell short, just brushing the other man backward, going full-length on the floor as a shot crashed out above him. Helplessly, he tensed for the shattering blow of a bullet between his unprotected shoulders. When it didn't come, he levered himself up, the Colt finally ready in his hand. Then he stopped, frozen, staring as the others in the room were staring at Garvey and Billy Troop.

Garvey stood upright, his Colt pointing at the ceiling. Troop's left hand held the lean cowhand's wrist so tightly that the flesh showed dead white under the pressure. Writhing in pain, Garvey rained left-handed blows on Troop's face and shoulders, but Troop simply ignored them. Without haste, he reached up and plucked the pistol away.

"You shouldn't have pulled a gun," he told Garvey carefully, as a man might correct an erring child. "I don't much like guns."

Then his left hand closed.

Above Garvey's agonized scream, Merritt heard the ugly crunch of bone. The next moment, Troop hurled the cowhand away from him. Garvey crashed into the corner between the bar and the wall and huddled there, cradling his injured wrist.

"Guess he don't need this," Troop said. He looked uncertainly at the gun, then laid it on the bar. "You want another beer, Yank?"

Merritt swept his eyes across the other customers, decided it was safe to holster his pistol. Before he could answer, a heavy stride hit the boardwalk outside and the saloon door slammed open. Marshal Bell stopped just inside the door. His square, farmer's hands held a stubby shotgun.

"Now, everybody just stand easy. What's going on here?"

There was silence except for Garvey's soft moans. "It was Troop," he grated. "That crazy Billy Troop. He tried to kill me."

"Um." Bell rubbed his chin and squinted at Troop. "Billy, you'd better come along with me. We'll see about this at the office."

"Just a minute, Marshal," Merritt said. "Billy was only helping me. It was my fault."

Bell sighed. "Mr. Merritt, I could very near have guessed that myself. What's your version of this?"

113

"Garvey pulled a gun. Billy took it away from him." Merritt jerked his head toward the crowd. "Everybody saw it, but I doubt they'll say so."

Bell looked at the saloonkeeper. "Cap?" he asked.

"All I saw was the Yank causing trouble. You just stand aside, Marshal, and we'll see he don't cause any more."

Bell's eyes went to Garvey again. He shrugged. "Seems to me some folks learn slow," he said to nobody in particular. "Couple of you fellers help Garvey over to Ma Sullivan's and see if she can set that arm." Then he gestured to Troop and Merritt. "All right, let's go."

The sound of the shot had stopped a few curious passersby in the street. They drew back cautiously as the three men came out of the saloon.

"Oh, for—" Bell mumbled. He raised his voice. "Nobody killed. Go home."

They began to drift away, but Laurie pushed her way through them to Merritt. Her face showed an almost comical mixture of anger and relief.

"Oh, Steve, I told you to stay out of there!" she said. "I heard the shot and I was afraid—" Conscious suddenly of the others listening, she stopped and her cheeks reddened.

Bell spoke to Billy Troop. "Billy, you know

where the jail is. Go on along. I want to talk to these folks."

"Sure, Marshal." Billy shambled away, pausing to look back at Merritt. "See you later, Yank."

"Look, Marshal," Merritt began. "If he's in any trouble—"

Bell ignored him. "I reckon if I lock this one up, you'll just bail him out," he said to Laurie.

"I suppose so."

"You better get him out of town, then. He don't act right bright."

"Thanks, Marshal," Merritt said.

Bell broke the shotgun and unloaded it, dropping the shells into his pocket. He looked thoughtfully after Billy Troop.

"Son, Billy came back from the War without much brains, but he's as good judging people as an old hound dog. If he likes you, I reckon you must be worth the trouble. Get along, now."

Bell turned away, and Laurie caught Merritt's arm impulsively. "Jory's already at the livery, along with the things I bought." She looked up at him. "What was it? What happened?"

"Nothing much," Merritt said. "But it looks like I've made a friend."

From what the marshal said, though, Billy

Troop wasn't likely to be much help. Still, it was a start. The way things were going, Merritt would need all the help he could find.

CHAPTER 8

Morning brought gray, low-lying clouds, borne by a cool wind and heavy with the promise of rain. It also brought Billy Troop. He was squatting comfortably on his heels, his back against the bunkhouse wall, when Merritt came out to go to breakfast.

"Morning, Yank," he called. He pushed back his forage cap and laughed like a pleased child at Merritt's surprise. "You don't look like you expected me."

"I didn't. How did you get here, anyway? Where did you leave your horse?"

"Oh, I walked out last night," Troop said. He looked down at his boots. "Some nights I don't sleep so good. I have dreams — you know."

"I know."

"Well, sometimes I'll get drunk, or get in a fight. Or I'll get out and maybe walk someplace. Last night, I taken a notion to come here."

Merritt shook his head, still half-believing

117

he was in some dream of his own. "But what about the marshal? You didn't — I mean, I thought he was going to hold you."

"Oh, he let me out soon's that Adam Garvey left town. Folks all know I'm crazy, anyway." He stood up and stretched. "You want to look out for that Adam Garvey. I don't much think he likes you."

"No," Merritt said. "I don't much think he does." He laughed. "Well, I'm glad to see you, Billy. Come up to the house, and we'll have some breakfast."

Merritt wasn't sure how Laurie would react to their unexpected guest, but she greeted Troop as if he dropped in for breakfast every day.

"Hello, Billy. Sit down, and I'll dish you up some eggs." She nodded toward Jory, who was already at the table. "Jory, you remember Mr. Troop. He helped your father last spring."

Jory stared with interest at Troop's battered face. Gulping a bite of biscuit, he said, "Morning, Mr. Troop. Morning, Steve."

"Howdy," Troop said. He sidled to the far end of the table and eased into a chair. "I guess I don't remember you, Jory. I don't remember too good, sometimes."

"I remember. Pa took us fishing when you finished."

Merritt drew up a chair while Laurie dished out eggs and biscuits and fried fatback and wild plum jam. When she'd finished, she took the seat at the head of the table and nudged Jory into saying a mumbled grace.

"Well, who should we pick a fight with today?" she asked brightly when he'd finished.

Merritt laughed. "Nobody, I hope. I thought I'd finish those stock pens Clint was building behind the barn. We'll need them when our army beef contracts come through."

"Oh." Laurie studied her plate. "Steve, even if the contracts come through, how are we going to fill them? We can't run this place without help."

Breaking off a whispered conversation with Jory, Billy Troop raised his head. He reached for another biscuit and spooned jam onto it, watching Merritt with innocent blue eyes.

"One thing at a time," Merritt said. "I had some ideas yesterday for finding hands. That'll work out."

Troop nodded profoundly and leaned to speak to Jory again. Merritt hardly noticed. Inside, he wasn't as sure of himself as he sounded. He was sure of one thing, though, now more than ever — no bunch of Rebs was going to run him out of here.

"Jory!" Laurie said sharply. "You know

119

you're not supposed to whisper at the table. Don't bother Mr. Troop."

Billy Troop smiled at her. "He ain't no bother, ma'am," he said. "Fact is, he was just going to ask you something."

He looked expectantly at Jory. The boy hesitated, then spoke in a rush.

"Well — when Pa took us fishing that other time, we found this pool with a great big old catfish, and Billy thought — we thought we could go catch him today if it's all right. Steve could come with us."

"Whoa," Merritt said. "Sorry, but I'd better get to work on those pens."

"Well, then, Billy and me. We'll bring back fish for supper. Please, Ma?"

"All right," Laurie agreed, and Merritt looked at her in surprise. "Just be sure your chores are done first. And be back for lunch."

"Sure, Ma. We'll do them now. C'mon, Billy."

Jory ran for the barn, banging the door behind him. More slowly, Troop got to his feet and followed. He paused in the doorway.

"Thank you kindly for the breakfast, ma'am," he said with self-conscious care. "Them biscuits were mighty fine."

Then he shambled out toward the barn, his head down, wide shoulders hunched as if he were expecting a blow. Watching him go,

Merritt shook his head.

"Laurie, are you sure you want Jory with him?" he asked. "He can be dangerous. He was like a big cat in that saloon. I've never seen a man his size move so fast."

"Billy?" Laurie stared at him in disbelief. "When he was out here helping Clint, he and Jory spent every spare minute together." She laughed. "I guess he could be dangerous, all right — to anything that threatened Jory."

Merritt nodded thoughtfully. He was beginning to believe there was more to Billy Troop than he'd first suspected.

By midmorning, he had staked out the sides of the pens and made a respectable start on the postholes. Clint had set a line of posts down one side — it was the last thing he'd worked on before he disappeared, Laurie said — but that was as far as he'd gotten. Cedar posts and rolls of the new-style wire he'd meant to use still lay in the barn. Now Merritt was working down the second long side, stopping occasionally to haul a bucket of water to moisten the ground for the chisel-pointed posthole diggers.

Jory could have helped with that, he thought, leaning on the handles while he mopped his face with a bandanna. He hadn't realized how much he'd come to depend on the boy's company, just as he'd come to depend on Laurie for a hundred things around the place. Probably too much, he thought. He was getting too involved with the two of them, and that couldn't be good. The whole thing was still just a business proposition.

"That's good, Yank," Billy Troop's voice said behind him. "Them's good deep postholes."

Startled, Merritt turned. Billy was standing by the corner of the barn. Jory joined him a moment later, struggling to carry a string of fair-sized catfish. The two of them had come up so quietly that Merritt hadn't noticed — and a good thing it hadn't been Frank or some of his friends, he thought.

"Thanks."

"Look, Steve." Jory held up the fish. "We didn't get the big one, but look. Ma can fix them for supper."

"That's a lot of fish for her to clean."

The boy made a face. "Oh, I'll have to do that. She won't clean fish, except her own. Do you want to help, Billy?"

Troop shook his head slightly. Taking that for his answer, Jory waved and went around to the kitchen door with his catch. Troop stayed where he was, looking with furrowed brow at the stakes and postholes.

"That's good," he said again. "But it ought

to go more up that way, toward the pump."

Merritt hadn't been listening. Now he straightened and looked at Troop.

"What?"

"Toward the pump. Then you could pump right into your water trough. I hate to haul water."

Merritt stared at the pump, then back at Troop. The big man was right. It would be simple enough to extend the pen and build a long watering trough along the end. In fact, it was obvious — now that Troop had mentioned it.

"You going to fix it right?" Billy asked.

"Yes." Merritt bit the answer off short. There was no reason to be angry with Troop. He stooped and began pulling up the stakes along that end. Troop watched for a few seconds, then took off his forage cap and hung it on a nail beside the barn door.

"Guess I'd just as well dig a hole or two."

Merritt looked up. "You don't have to do that, Billy," he said.

"Oh, it's no trouble. Mr. Culver, he says I work good. I do jobs for him some, and sleep in his stable."

Troop had already picked up the posthole diggers. The muscles of his back and shoulders bunching, he drove the points powerfully into the dry soil and scooped out a big bite of earth. Merritt whistled as the tool came down a second time.

"Well, if you get tired of working for him, let me know," he said. "I think we could use you around here."

The big man grunted, but didn't answer. Merritt watched a little longer, then shrugged and turned back to his work. He was glad of the help, and he could easily correct any mistakes Troop might make.

In the time it took Merritt to finish the staking, Troop had extended the row of postholes all the way to the corner of the pens. Then, apparently tiring of the job, he went to reclaim his forage cap.

"Hey, Yank, maybe I could take your wagon," he said. "I gotta go back to town. Looks like it's about to rain."

"Well, sure, Billy." Merritt looked regretfully at the line of holes Troop had dug, and the amount of work that remained. "I can drive you in. Or, if you want to wait until after lunch—"

Troop shook his head. "No. Let me take your wagon. I'll see it gets back safe."

After a moment's hesitation, Merritt agreed. He couldn't guess what was on Troop's mind, and digging it out would be a lot of trouble.

Anyway, he was beginning to trust the big Reb. Troop turned without another word and went into the barn, and Merritt returned to his digging. He'd just started setting the first corner post when he heard the clatter of the wagon pulling out, but he was too busy to do more than glance up. Probably, he thought, Troop would forget all about the wagon, and they'd have to pick it up in town. It was strange. Sometimes Troop made perfect sense, and sometimes he seemed more of a child than Jory. Still, it would have been nice to keep him around for a while — at least until the corral posts were set.

That afternoon, the rain that had held off for so long began to fall. Merritt straightened and pulled off his hat, letting the cool mist sweep over him. When the first big drops came, he quickly gathered the tools into the barn, then strolled through the cool rain toward the house. Laurie met him at the door, holding a dry dish towel out to him.

"Here. I thought Yankees were smart enough to come in out of the rain, but you're soaked. Dry off." Then she dropped her lecturing tone and laughed. "Oh, but think how it'll help the grass!"

Toweling his face and hair, Merritt grinned. "Even better, it gave me an excuse to quit for the day." He stretched to flex his shoulders. "This is a lot more work than most business managers do."

To his surprise, Laurie's laughter died away. She took a step toward him, looking up into his face.

"I know," she said. She put a hand on his arm. "I'm always saying this, but we – I – owe you a lot, Steve. Thank you."

Her eyes were level and honest as always, but with a trace of a new expression, a softness he hadn't noticed there before.

"Laurie," he began. Then a long roll of thunder, deep and clear as the growl of distant artillery, went through the clouds overhead. He moved away to the porch railing and looked out into the rain.

"It's really coming down out there. Is Jory inside someplace?"

"Didn't you know? He went to town with Billy." Laurie came to stand near him, not touching. "I expect they'll wait there until it blows over."

Leaning forward across the rail, Merritt stiffened. "We're having company anyway. Look."

A rider was coming up the trail toward the house, his head bowed into the rain. A yellow waterproof covered his head and shoulders.

Merritt dropped his hand to the Colt at his side, then realized its powder was probably wet from the rain. A long stride took him to the door of the cabin and he reached inside for the Spencer.

"It's all right," Laurie called. "It's Marshal Bell."

Merritt straightened, leaving the carbine in its place beside the door. Laurie looked up at him as he came back to stand beside her.

"What do you think he wants? If it's about that business at the saloon—"

"We'll find out soon enough," Merritt said.

Bell dismounted in the yard and led his horse into the shelter of the barn. After a couple of minutes, he squelched through the mud to the porch steps.

"Come inside, Marshal," Laurie greeted him. "You need to dry out. I'll make some coffee."

"Oh, no, ma'am." Bell took off his hat and slapped it against his thigh. "I wouldn't track up your house. I just wanted a word with Mr. Merritt here — in private, if you don't mind."

"Of course." Laurie took a step toward the door, then stopped. She turned a hard, level gaze on the marshal. "It's about Clint, isn't it?" she said. Then, quickly: "Have you found him?"

"No." The marshal hesitated, twisting his hat

in his hands. "No, ma'am, it isn't that at all."

"Tell me." When he didn't answer, she added, "I have a right to hear it, whatever it is."

Merritt had never seen Bell look unsure of himself, but now the marshal's face showed signs of some sort of struggle going on inside.

"I expect you're right, ma'am," he said at last. "But probably you ain't heard the − ah, the gossip about Clint and − how he might have went away."

"About Mary Beth Rankin, you mean?" Laurie's laugh was short and sharp. She shook her head pityingly. "Marshal, I knew about her the first day I came out here. Half a dozen well-meaning ladies just couldn't wait to tell me."

"I see." Bell rubbed his chin while he thought about that. Then he shrugged out of the slicker and draped it over the porch railing. "I reckon a cup of coffee might be just the thing, ma'am," he said.

Seated at the table, Bell seemed more at ease. He sipped from the steaming mug of coffee Laurie had given him and made an appreciative face.

"Thank you kindly, ma'am," he said. "What I come about, the deputy down in San Antonio found Clint's horse − that big chestnut gelding. I figured he'd turn up."

"His horse?" Laurie looked puzzled. "But what—"

"Who was riding him?" Merritt asked at the same time.

"A Mexican gent, Don Jorge something. Swore he'd bought the horse down on the border just about the time Clint dropped out of sight. Said he'd paid fifty gold pesos to a gringo with a beard, and he had a bill of sale to prove it. The bill of sale was signed with an 'X.'"

"But—" Laurie shook her head. "I don't understand. What about Clint?"

"Nothing about him. That's why I didn't want to tell you straight out. The feller Don Jorge described sure wasn't Clint, and the trail's dead cold by now."

"How about the Rankin girl?" Merritt put in. "Did Don Jorge mention her?"

"No-o." Bell glanced apologetically at Laurie. Her lips tightened a little, but she gave no other sign. "Way I see it, there's two things could have happened. Either her and Clint ran for the border and they sold the horse right away, or else somebody else had the horse from the start."

"Then Clint never left," Laurie said. Her voice was dull. "He's dead, Marshal. We'd have heard from him if he wasn't."

"Now, we don't know that, ma'am. All the same, I think Frank and me will look around the county a little harder."

Laurie shook her head. "I know, if you don't." She rose from her place. "There's only one thing you can do now. Find out who killed him — and why."

Her voice had broken on the last word. She stood very still for a moment, then turned and walked to the doorway of the bedroom.

"I'm sorry," she whispered. "Steve, see the marshal out when he's finished."

The door closed behind her. Bell sat for a time, staring at it thoughtfully. Then he drained his cup and set it on the table.

"Listen, Marshal," Merritt said. "I want to do something about this. Maybe I could follow up on that horse — or I could talk to the Rankin family."

Bell chuckled. "I think you'd do better to leave it to us," he said mildly. He looked again at the door. "Seems to me you've got all you can handle without taking up manhunting."

He pushed back his chair and stood up.

"Looks like the rain's stopped. I'll go along now. If we hear any more about Clint, I'll let you know first thing."

Merritt walked with him to the barn. It was growing dark now, and the rain clouds were

130

breaking up before a cold east wind. Bell spread his slicker over his shoulders. Lifting his head, he snuffed at the air like an old bear.

"Cold snap coming," he commented. He untied his horse and hauled himself into the saddle. "Thought you might like to know Baldy Witherspoon's back in town. He's still got that long Sharps."

"Thanks," Merritt said. He smiled grimly. "It seems like two or three folks around here are taking a special interest in me. I don't guess I'll have to worry about Garvey for a while, though."

"It's his brains you need to worry about, not his arm," Bell said. "Always wondered why he never got past sergeant in that Home Guard outfit. But he's a mean one." He clucked to his horse. "Say my good-byes to Laurie," he called back over his shoulder. Then, so low Merritt barely heard, "That's some woman."

Merritt watched from the doorway of the barn until the marshal was out of sight. Inside the house, Laurie was alone. She'd been close to tears, upset by the marshal's news. He knew he should go in to her, for talk or comfort or whatever she needed, but still he held back. Standing there, he realized how long it had been since he'd thought of anything to do with his old life. Even Elizabeth now seemed more like a dream than a real woman he'd loved. Maybe that was all she'd ever been, he thought — a dream he could turn to between battles, when he had nothing else. Those dreams were over, though. He couldn't afford to start on another.

Slowly, Merritt crossed the yard to the bunkhouse. He lighted the lamp, then sat down and began to disassemble the Navy Colt. He cleaned the weapon carefully, more carefully than necessary, and then reloaded it. He was just finishing up when he heard the spring wagon waddling back from town. Slipping the pistol into its holster, he went outside. Troop had brought the wagon up in front of the barn. To Merritt's surprise, the butter-churn bay he'd rented from Sid Culver trailed at the tailboard.

"Oh. Howdy, Yank," Troop said. "Didn't see you there." He climbed down, passing the reins to Jory. "Anything wrong? You don't look so good."

"It's nothing, Billy."

Merritt didn't feel like talking about it, especially not to Troop. Instead, he said, "Billy? Where'd this horse come from?"

Troop was unloading bundles of something from the wagon. "Oh, he's mine," he said. "Mr. Culver, he owed me for some work, so I took the horse for pay. I figured I better bring him along when I brought my gear."

"Brought your — what do you mean?"

Troop looked around at Merritt in surprise. "I didn't have a horse," he explained carefully. "But you said I could work here if I wanted to, so I had to have one. I brought him out when I brought my gear." He held up a battered war bag. "I thought about it, Yank," he added. "I figured I better work for you. We ought to stick together, you and me — we're the same kind of folks. See?"

Merritt stared at him. Then, all at once, he began to laugh. Sometimes the things Troop said made a kind of sense. Well, he'd been wanting a hired hand. Now, it looked as if he had one.

"I see now, Billy," he said. "Sometimes I guess I'm not too smart." He reached up to take the lines from Jory. "Put your things in the bunkhouse. Jory and I can tend to the horses."

"Boy, Steve," Jory said as they led the team into the barn. "Aren't we lucky Billy decided to stay?"

"We sure are, old-timer," Merritt said. Then the laughter drained away from him. Almost to himself, he added, "Maybe it'll give me time to look into some things I've been wondering about."

CHAPTER 9

Merritt reined up at the crest of the hill over-looking Tom Drake's ranch and waited. Billy Troop was a couple of hundred yards behind, just starting up out of the valley. Merritt's horse threw up its head and snorted, then edged forward against the pull of the reins. Gently, with bit and knees, he quieted the animal.

"Easy, boy. We'll just wait here for a minute."

The horse was a shaggy dun stallion, not much to look at, but good with cattle. Merritt had bought him from Sid Culver two weeks before — probably paying more than he was worth, he thought — and the two of them had come to know each other well.

Sitting upright in the saddle, Merritt flexed his aching back and shoulders. He'd thought he was in good condition, but the past days had shown him how wrong he'd been. He and Troop had finished the cattle pens, then set out to round up the scattered cows wearing the LJ brand.

"We can handle them better if they're all together," he'd told Laurie. "That little valley you showed me would be a good place — there's plenty of grass and water. Maybe that'll stop them from straying into somebody else's herd."

That had been Merritt's real introduction to ranching. He'd spent more hours in the saddle than any time since the War, going out with Troop in the gray dawn and coming home long after the stars were out. There were only a couple of hundred head on the ranch, but they were scattered and range-wise, the cows fiercely determined to protect their new calves. They had to be hazed out of the dense brush in ones and twos, then driven down to the valley. It had taken ten days before Laurie came out to help them move the last big bunch from Phantom Hill.

Halfway through, Merritt had begun to realize he could never have done it without Billy Troop. Tireless and always cheerful, Troop had shown a knowledge of cattle and a mastery of horse and lariat that astonished Merritt. He'd even found time to drag out the big walking plow and break up half an acre so Laurie could get in a belated garden.

"That plowing's all right," he said. "No hurry, and it gives you time to think. Like fishing."

Now, leaning on his saddle horn and watching Troop ride up to join him, Merritt again shook his head in wonder.

"Billy, I think you could wear down an ammunition mule," he said. "Don't you ever get tired?"

Troop brought the bay up and stopped. He sat for a moment with shoulders hunched before answering.

"Wasn't my idea to work today. Jory and me was going fishing. I figure we got enough cows for just us to nurse."

"Maybe, but half of them are steers," Merritt said. "What we buy from Mr. Drake will help us build the herd — cows with calves, or heifers that'll calve next year."

Troop shrugged. "Fine feller, Mr. Drake," he said. "I like him. Got a nice place, too."

Merritt nodded. Spread out below them, Drake's ranch headquarters showed the results of care and planning. The stone house was small and solid. Barn, corrals, and branding chute were well built and in good repair, and a fenced pasture behind them held a dozen horses. It was a layout someone had put a lot of work into, and a lot of pride.

Four men were gathered in front of the barn. Three of them stood in a circle around Tom Drake, who knelt in the center. As Troop and

Merritt rode up, the rancher straightened, brushing dust from his knees.

"Morning." Drake stumped over toward them, a smile creasing his leathery face. "Didn't figure you'd be here so early. Light down until I get these boys lined out, and then we'll talk."

Merritt smiled in return, but kept his place in the saddle, looking past Drake at the three cowhands. They had come a couple of steps closer, and now stood in a line a few yards behind their boss. The one in the center was Adam Garvey.

Seeing the direction of Merritt's gaze, Drake glanced back. As he did so, Garvey took a step nearer.

"It's all right, Yank. I ain't looking for trouble today." His mouth twisted into a wry smile, and he held up his right arm. The wrist was crudely splinted and held to his chest by a makeshift sling. "Couldn't make much if I wanted to."

"That's enough, Adam," Drake said sharply. "Why don't you and Slim get on over to that water hole by the red bluff. We need it cleaned out."

"Why, sure, Mr. Drake." Garvey's eyes didn't leave Merritt's face. "I'll be seeing you, Yank."

"Anytime."

Merritt held his position until Garvey and

one of the others had mounted and ridden out. Then he stepped down from the saddle and offered Drake his hand.

"Sorry I was so long in getting here. I hope you've still got some cattle to sell."

Drake pushed back his hat. "No danger I wouldn't, I'm afraid. I've got some out in the back pasture for you to look at." He motioned to the third of the cowhands. "Jim Bob, come over here a minute."

Merritt hadn't really noticed either of the men flanking Garvey. This one, he saw, was barely more than a boy — sixteen, maybe, with a shadow of moustache on his lip and the slender wiriness of a lynx in his movement.

"Jim Bob's my youngest boy," Drake said. "His brothers is off down by Waco, running a store. It's just him and me at home since his ma died."

"Glad to meet you, Jim Bob," Merritt said.

"Howdy." The boy's eyes were interested and not especially hostile. He took no notice of Merritt's outstretched hand, reaching instead for the dun's reins. "I'll see to your horses. Reckon you all and Pa will want to talk some business."

Drake led the way through a gate and down a rutted path, Merritt and Troop trailing along behind. Soon they came to another fenced enclosure, this one maybe forty acres in extent. Perhaps a hundred head of cattle and half that many calves milled aimlessly behind the wire. Even to Merritt's untrained eye, they were stockier and more compact than the rangy longhorns he and Billy had been chasing for the past weeks.

"A lot of these have Durham blood," Drake said. "I tried some crossbreeding back before the War. Brought over two bulls and twenty heifers." He chuckled. "I should've known better — those old range bulls killed my shorthorn bulls first week. But the heifers did fine."

Merritt nodded. "I've seen Durhams in the East," he said. "Looks like they carry more weight of beef, but will they stand the climate?"

"They're still here. These are mostly longhorn, of course. I ain't had much chance to work with breeding since the War." He cleared his throat. "How many were you thinking about?"

Merritt looked over at Billy Troop, who was leaning against the fence watching the calves.

"Billy? What about it?"

"They'll do fine. I herded them some. Not as mean as them full-blood longhorns."

"All right," Merritt said. "I can handle about seventy-five head right now. Maybe later we'll want more, if you're still willing to sell."

Drake rubbed his mouth with the back of his hand. "That's fine. Now, I was figuring eight dollars a head for cows with calves, and seven for the heifers."

Billy Troop moved a little at Merritt's side, then settled his elbows back on the fence post and gazed raptly toward the pasture. Merritt shook his head.

"I'll give you three dollars apiece for the lot," he said.

Tom Drake's head jerked around toward Merritt, but the rancher quickly hid his surprise. He tugged at the brim of his hat and studied the ground at Merritt's feet.

"That's hard lines, Mr. Merritt," he said at last. "You know I'm anxious to sell, but that's a rock-bottom price to offer a neighbor."

"That's right," Merritt agreed. "And eight dollars is 'way over the market around here. That's not much of a price to offer a neighbor, either — unless he's a greenhorn Yankee."

For a moment, Drake was silent. Then he chuckled, and the lines around his eyes deepened with amusement.

"That's the honest truth, Mr. Merritt — and I'm sorry for it. I guess I've got caught by my own rope."

"Maybe not," Merritt said. "Let's say five for the heifers and five and a half for the others —

and we pick them out. That strikes me as a good, neighborly price."

Drake stuck out his hand. "Mr. Merritt, you have a deal." He jerked his head toward the pen. "You and Billy go right ahead. I'll get Jim Bob and some of the boys to help you cut them out and move them to your range."

He trudged away toward the house. Watching him, Billy Troop spat reflectively on the ground.

"You did good there, Yank," he said. "That was right nice."

Merritt snorted. "Nothing nice about it, Billy," he said. "We'll need to deal with him later. There's no point in making another enemy. We still got a good price."

The expression smoothed out of Troop's face, leaving it blank and impartial. "I wouldn't never have thought of it that way," he said. "Guess that was mighty clever of you."

Something in his tone made Merritt look at him sharply, but the big man had already turned away to study the animals in the corral.

Selecting the cows and cutting them out took most of the day, even with the help of Jim Bob and two of Drake's hands. Merritt made the choices himself, sometimes asking Troop's advice. The cattle were strong and fat from the spring grass, and Merritt was satisfied they'd be a good addition to the LJ herd. When the job was done, he left Billy and the others to get the cows started on the trail, while he rode back to Drake's ranch house. He found the rancher just coming in from the barn.

"We're just getting ready to move out," he said. "Do you want to look them over?"

"Nope. I'll trust you." Drake gestured toward the house. "Step inside here, and I'll draw you up a bill of sale."

The inside of the house was as trim and neat as the outside. Merritt waited while Drake washed up, and then the rancher opened a cupboard and took down a big green ledger.

"I keep most of my accounts here," he said. He dipped the pen and wrote in small, careful letters, then tore off half the page for Merritt. "Here you are."

"Thanks. If I can use that pen, I'll write you a draft to Mr. Whitlock."

He handed over the draft, then preceded Drake out onto the porch. As he stepped down into the yard, he suddenly remembered something the marshal had said earlier.

"By the way, does a man called Jud Rankin live near here?"

Drake paused with his hand on the porch railing. The smile on his face suddenly vanished.

"The Rankin place is just up the road a piece." Drake pointed. "Over northwest, maybe two miles." He hesitated, then said, "If you don't mind my asking, what's your business with Jud Rankin?"

"Nothing much," Merritt said, surprised. "I just thought I might ride by and meet him. Why?"

"Well—" Drake took off his hat and wiped his forehead, then put the hat back on. "Old Jud, he's a mite cantankerous. I thought you might've had some trouble with him."

"No, nothing like that. His daughter was supposed to be mixed up with Clint somehow. I wanted to talk to him about it."

The rancher frowned, his face showing a worry Merritt found hard to understand. "Clint's been gone a good while, Mr. Merritt. Some things are better left alone."

"Well, I don't mean to leave this one alone. Sooner or later, I'm going to find out what happened to him."

Drake sighed and looked down at his hands. "Mr. Merritt," he began, but then the sound of a horse coming up the track behind Merritt interrupted him. Merritt looked around as Jim Bob pulled up in the yard.

"They're ready to move, Pa," the boy said.

"All right, son, take them along." Whatever

Drake had been about to say, he'd obviously changed his mind. "You mind that you and the boys come straight back from Mr. Merritt's, hear? Don't go stopping off in town."

The boy laughed and reined his horse around. "Sure, Pa," he said.

He spurred the animal back the way he'd come. Merritt looked at Drake a moment longer, then mounted and waved a hand to him. The rancher didn't reply. When Merritt looked back, Drake was still watching him from the porch, his face troubled.

Halfway down the trail to the pasture, Merritt fell in beside Jim Bob.

"Can you and Billy handle the herd without me for a while?" he asked.

The boy gave him a look of mingled scorn and amusement. "Oh, I reckon we can manage."

"Good. Tell Billy I'll be along presently. I have something to do at the Rankin place."

The Rankins lived in a picket cabin, built of vertical slabs of rough-cut oak. The roof was a canvas wagon sheet tied down at the corners and covered with crude thatching. Merritt remembered such quarters from his first hitch in the Army. They were easy and quick to build, but he knew the roof would leak and the uncured pickets would warp, leaving gaps for the cold winds of winter. It was a poor enough place, and he thought dispassionately that a man should be able to do better.

He rode in slowly, dismounted in the bare and open yard between the cabin and the barn. He looked for a place to tie the dun, then let the reins drop.

"Hello!" he called. "Jud Rankin?"

"Who's that?" The answer came hoarsely from behind the house. Merritt waited in the sun until the man limped around the corner to face him. "Here I be. Who're you?"

Rankin was the far side of forty, Merritt guessed, tall and stringy, with a slab-sided jaw and suspicious brown eyes. His daughter must have gotten her looks someplace else.

"Well?"

"My name's Merritt, Mr. Rankin. I wanted to talk to you—"

"Yeah, you're that Yankee. I been hearing about you. What do you want?"

Merritt paused, weighing the man. Rankin didn't look too sensitive, but people had funny ideas about family matters. There wasn't going to be any easy way to do this.

"I'm looking for Clint Davidson," he said. "The marshal told me Clint and Mary Beth disappeared about the same time. I thought you might know something that would help find them."

"Ain't no reason I should tell you, if'n I did." Rankin scratched his stubbled chin. "Still, it's no secret. She took out one night back in the winter with our old mare and all the money we had at the place. Good riddance, except now my woman don't have anybody to help her."

Merritt stood silent for a minute, waiting, listening to the raucous cry of a mockingbird from the mesquite tree beside the cabin. Finally, Rankin went on.

"I been meaning to go and look for her. Reckon she'd find her way to one of them hog ranches down around San Antone. She was always wild, and I couldn't whip it out of her."

"About Clint—" Merritt began, but a voice from the house interrupted him.

"Jud Rankin!" A woman came to the door. "There's chores to do! You quit— Why, who's that?" She came through the low doorway, smoothing out her apron. "You never said we had company."

"This here's the Yankee from over to Davidson's. He's asking about Mary Beth and Clint."

"The Yankee? Well, I swan." She came nearer, peering nearsightedly at Merritt. "We ain't heard from Mary since she left. I'm feared something's happened to her." She shook her head sadly. "And her so pretty, too. Just shows how the devil can get into a child."

"Do you think she was going with Clint?" Merritt prodded gently. "Did you ever see her with him?"

"I'd of filled his butt with buckshot if I had," Rankin growled. He spat in the dust. "Still, there was always some man or other sniffing after her. If Clint didn't cover her, I guess he was about the only one in the county she missed."

Rankin looked up slyly at Merritt, his mouth pulling into an ugly grin.

"Anyway, I doubt Clint was getting what he wanted from that uppity little wife of his — but I guess you'd know more about that than me."

Without thinking, Merritt shot out a hand, grabbed Rankin by his shirtfront. He shoved the other man back hard against the flimsy pickets of the cabin, his fist poised to strike.

"Listen, you—"

"What's the matter with you? I didn't mean nothing! I didn't mean nothing!"

Rankin's face was pale under its coating of dirt. He stared up at Merritt with a mixture of surprise and fear in his wide eyes. Merritt looked at him for a moment, then unclenched his fist. Disgusted, he released the homesteader and turned away. Breaking Rankin's jaw wouldn't help the search for Clint, or Laurie's reputation. It would just cause more talk.

Rankin sagged back against the wall, glowering at Merritt. Before he could speak, his wife planted herself in front of him, hands on her hips.

"Jud Rankin!" the woman snapped. "I'd be ashamed, saying such a thing! And him looking for Mary Beth, which is more than her own pa's done."

"Reckon she can find her own way back, if she's of a mind," Rankin said sullenly. He lurched upright, pointing an unsteady finger at Merritt. "I got chores to do, mister. You get off my land or I'll have the law on you."

He turned his back, limping around the corner of the house. His wife watched him go, then took a couple of steps out toward Merritt.

"You'll tell me if you hear anything?" She was almost whispering, looking nervously the way Rankin had gone. "We never got along good with Mary, but I'd purely like to hear she's well."

"I'll let you know," Merritt said. "Thanks for your help." He caught the dun's reins and mounted. He could ask more questions, but that probably wouldn't help him now. "If you remember anything else, I'd appreciate your telling me."

The woman glanced quickly in the direction Rankin had gone. She lowered her voice. "I will. I'll get you word some way. But you better get along now."

Merritt turned the dun's head and rode back up the weed-choked lane from the cabin. Brush and mesquite closed in on both sides, blocking his view at each bend. A ground squirrel skittered across in front of him, and cicadas droned busily among the thick leaves. Thinking about his talk with Rankin, he hardly noticed his surroundings until he was almost to the main road. Then he heard the soft whicker of another horse and drew rein abruptly. A rider had just turned up the lane toward the Rankin place.

Putting down one hand to quiet the dun, he drew the Spencer carbine from its scabbard and rested it across the saddlebow. Rankin was just the type to circle around on him. If it was anyone else, he could always apologize. At least he'd be alive to talk about it.

The sounds came closer, until Frank Harmon rounded the corner, pulling his horse up short and hard when he saw the dun. Surprise and quick anger showed in the deputy's face.

"Look out! What do you think—?"

Then he recognized Merritt and his hand dropped to his pistol. Merritt raised the carbine.

"Don't do it, Frank. The marshal will need a new deputy."

Harmon scowled, but moved his hand away. "Most folks around here don't pull a gun on everybody they meet, Yank. You'll get killed like that, one of these days."

"Sorry, Frank." Merritt brought the Spencer up and rested it in the crook of his arm with the muzzle pointing away from Harmon. "Somebody tried to bushwhack me not long ago. I don't intend it to happen again."

"Seems like you can't stay out of trouble, Merritt. But then, people just don't like a stranger moving in and taking advantage of a lone woman — especially some carpetbagging bluebelly."

This time, Merritt felt more surprise than anger. He'd known there must be some reason for Frank's hostility, something more than just his being a Northerner. Now he thought he knew what it was.

"I don't have any hold on Laurie, if that's what you mean," he said. "And after your visit to the ranch the other night, I'd guess you don't either — if you ever did."

The deputy's face flushed. He started an angry reply, but it died unspoken. He was looking past Merritt now, down the trail toward the Rankin place. His expression changed suddenly, as if he'd just remembered something.

"What are you doing here?" he demanded.

The abrupt question caught Merritt by surprise. He'd almost forgotten his anger, but now it came back in a rush. "Just visiting with a neighbor," he snapped.

"You stay away from Jud Rankin. This is county business, not yours. What did he tell you?"

"Suppose you ask him."

Frank kneed his horse closer, crowding Merritt in the narrow trail. "Listen, Yank, I'm tired of your smart answers. If you—"

The tone and the crowding finally snapped Merritt's temper. He hadn't punched Jud Rankin because Rankin was such a pitiful specimen, but that objection didn't apply to Frank.

"And I'm tired of being told what to do by some tinhorn with a badge," he cut in coldly. "Why don't you step out from behind that badge and gun for a few minutes?"

The deputy stared at him. Then a wry smile tugged at his mouth. "Yeah," he said. "That may be just the thing. Right here all right?"

Merritt nodded. Harmon reached up slowly to unpin his badge. He swung down from his horse and stood looking up at Merritt.

"All right, Yank. Put that cannon away."

"Uh-uh. You go first."

Almost automatically, Frank reached for the

151

buckle of his gun belt. Then he froze, his hands clenching and unclenching, his eyes still on Merritt. The thought in them was so clear that Merritt laughed aloud.

"Standoff," he said.

"Maybe not."

Frank moved his hand toward his gun again, watching Merritt. Merritt tightened his grip on the carbine. All at once, he realized how far he'd have to swing around to line the gun up on Harmon. Frank had gained an advantage, and he knew it. His eyes were steady on Merritt's, confident and unafraid. He's fast with a gun, Merritt thought, maybe fast enough to win against a stacked deck. Anyway, he's going to try.

Then the tense silence was broken by a crashing from back toward the road and a hoarse yell.

"Hey, Yank!"

With a tremendous surge of relief, Merritt grinned. "In here, Billy."

Billy Troop rode around the corner and stopped, almost touching Frank. "Right crowded in here," he observed mildly.

Harmon looked at Troop, then back at Merritt. He laughed suddenly, a harsh bark with little amusement in it.

"That was close, Yank. Maybe next time."

Mounting his horse, he brushed roughly past Merritt and rode on toward the Rankin house. Merritt let out a long breath.

"Billy, I'm surely glad to see you," he said. Then he frowned. "But what are you doing here?"

"Oh, Jim Bob told me where you were going. I figured I better come look after you."

"I don't need—" Merritt began irritably, but then he stopped. "Well, maybe I do. Let's ride, before Frank gets through with his visit."

CHAPTER 10

"Hey, Yank."

Merritt paused in the doorway of the general store, wrestling with the armload of bundles that he carried. When he'd first come to Gilead, he thought fleetingly, that call would have been a challenge. Now he was accustomed to it. The townspeople — most of them, anyway — seemed to accept his being there. He was still "the Yank" to them, though, and he realized again how completely that name set him apart.

"Yes, ma'am?"

Grace Evans, the storekeeper's gray-haired wife, held up a long envelope. "I almost forgot," she said. "The mail coach left this for you." She squinted disapprovingly at the address. "Must be important. It's from the Yankee government."

Merritt put the boxes down with a thump and came quickly over. "Commissary Officer, Fort Richardson, Department of Texas," he read.

"Thanks, Mrs. Evans. I've been waiting for this."

"Hmph. Good news, I hope."

"I hope so, too. Thank you again."

He stuck the letter in his pocket, to the woman's obvious disappointment. Gathering up his purchases, he went out to the waiting wagon. Jory, perched on the wagon box sucking a piece of horehound candy, cocked an eye at him.

"You took a long time. Billy and me are going fishing when we get back."

"You two will catch every fish in that river if you don't look out," Merritt said absently. He dumped the bundles into the back of the wagon, then eagerly tore into the letter.

"Who's that from?" Jory asked.

"The Army." Merritt ran his eye quickly down the page. "Major George Summers. I knew him in the War — he must've stayed in."

"What's he want?"

"Two hundred head — delivered Fort Richardson by—" Merritt whistled. "That's less than three weeks. Payment of seven-fifty—" Abruptly, he folded the paper. "Looks like the fishing will have to wait. We just sold some cattle."

"Good!" Jory bounced on the seat, grinning. "Ma will like that. Can we have a party?"

155

"We'll have a party when we're finished. Right now, I'd better talk to Mr. Whitlock."

Two hours later, he pulled the wagon up before the ranch house and climbed down, tossing the reins to Jory. Laurie, hearing the noise, had come out on the porch to meet them.

"What happened to you two?" she asked. "I expected you back an hour ago. Lunch—"

Merritt leaped up on the porch and danced her around, while Jory laughed delightedly.

"Never mind lunch. Where's Billy?"

"Why, he rode out to check on the herd. He's only been gone a little while." She pulled away, looking from him to Jory. "Have you both gone completely crazy?"

"Probably." Merritt pushed the letter into her hand. "Here, we're in business. Two hundred head. We have about eighty culls — steers and barren cows — and Banker Whitlock says he'll line up the rest. And some help to drive them."

"Oh!" She read the letter over quickly, then looked up at him. "Fort Richardson. That's almost a hundred miles."

Merritt laughed. "Well, it's not much of a trail drive, but it'll do— What is it?" She had turned away, facing toward the river and the plains, her hands clenched on the porch railing. Merritt went to her, put his hands on her

156

shoulders. "What's the matter, Laurie? I thought you'd be pleased. It means we're starting to pay our way. The ranch—"

"Yes." She straightened, then turned to face him. "That's what matters, isn't it — the ranch?" She smiled, but there was something like disappointment in her voice. "I am pleased, Steve. You'd better go tell Billy. We'll have a lot of work to do."

She squeezed his arm, then slipped past him into the house. Merritt stood for a moment on the porch, looking after her. Then, slowly, he went down the steps and crossed to the barn. She was right. He'd better find Billy Troop. They would have a lot to do.

Moving the beeves into the stock pen near the house was an easier job than Merritt had anticipated, but it still occupied several days. Laurie took a deep interest in the details of the drive and the chances of a regular contract, and Merritt decided she'd gotten over her initial reaction. She also, he noted, seemed to have forgotten her aversion to Yankee money.

Merritt did worry a little about the banker's part of the deal. He trusted Whitlock — within reason — but he knew how many things could go wrong when you depended on other people. He half-expected trouble the day he and Billy, driving a last dozen head of bawling longhorns down to the pens, topped the ridge to see Whitlock's surrey waiting in front of the house.

"Looks like that banker feller," Billy Troop said suspiciously. "Reckon what he wants out here?"

"He was doing a little business for me, Billy."

Merritt's dun interrupted, racing to head off a straying cow. Merritt chivyed the animal back to the herd, then fell in beside Troop again.

"I hope he's here to tell me it's finished. We need to start moving beef pretty soon, if we're going to fill that contract."

Troop grunted. "You're starting to learn about this cowboying business. That banker, though, you want to watch him. He looks out for himself."

Merritt grinned and urged the dun ahead a little. "I'll try," he said. "Let's get this bunch in the pen, and see what he has to say."

Banker Whitlock was still sitting in his surrey, and Laurie had come out onto the porch to talk with him. She stood at ease, one arm around a post, and she looked up and smiled as Merritt approached. It was dusk, the sun showing round and red through a low bank of clouds. Merritt noticed for the first time that the light brought out golden highlights in her brown hair.

"Ah, Mr. Merritt." Whitlock hesitated, then

somewhat reluctantly offered his hand. Merritt scrubbed his palm on his trouser leg. "We were just talking about you. I can see you have the place in fine shape."

"Thanks," Merritt said. He glanced again at Laurie, then back at the banker. "Sorry I haven't had time to clean up. Would you like to come in for some coffee?"

"Oh, no. Your — that is, Laurie already asked me. I must get along directly. I just wanted to tell you that everything is in readiness. I've managed to line up one hundred fifty head at Jim Bouldin's place, just a few miles from your destination. That should save you a great deal of trouble."

Merritt looked at him in surprise. "That's true, but it won't help the economy around here much. I thought you'd pick them up locally."

"It's good business for you, and that's good business for me," Whitlock said. He reached into a small satchel, drew out some papers. "The price at Bouldin's will be four dollars a head. If you'll sign this, you can pay with a note of hand to the banker in Jacksboro. I've already made the arrangements."

"Good." Merritt glanced over the document, then scrawled his name at the bottom. "Now, about some hands to help with the drive—"

The banker held up a hand. "I took the liberty of making an arrangement with Mr. Ben Allgood. He and his two sons will be here at sundown tomorrow. They've agreed to work for two dollars a day per man for as long as you need them."

"Well—" Merritt frowned doubtfully. "They're good men? I expected trouble getting anybody."

"The Allgood place is some distance from town, and they're rather independent," Whitlock said. He smiled again. "Also, this will improve their credit rating substantially. You can rely on them."

"I see," Merritt said. "You've thought of everything, I guess."

"Just doing my job." Whitlock handed Merritt some folded papers and an envelope. "Here's a map of the route to Bouldin's — though I'm sure Ben Allgood knows the way — and a letter of introduction. If that's all satisfactory, I'll be going."

"Fine," Merritt said. Then he shook himself. "Ah — would you like me to ride a little way with you? It'll be full dark before you get back to town."

Whitlock spread his hands. "Oh, no thanks. I'm perfectly safe." Reaching into the floorboard of the surrey, he brought up a sawed-off shotgun and laid it on the seat beside him.

160

"When I first came here, there was one attempt to rob me. Since then, I've had no problems." He tipped his hat politely to Laurie. "Good evening, ma'am. Mr. Merritt."

"Good evening."

Merritt watched the banker drive away. Looking up at Laurie, he whistled. "I think Billy's right about that man," he said. "He looks after himself."

"I don't like him," Laurie said simply. "Still, he's a good businessman. Clint trusted him."

Billy Troop came around the corner from the bunkhouse, still toweling his face. "He gone?" he asked. "I'm sure ready for some supper."

Laurie laughed. "All right. Steve, you'd better get cleaned up. Supper in two shakes."

Ben Allgood looked to be in his fifties, a lean, muscular man with a prophet's beard. He and his sons came riding into the wagonyard at midafternoon the next day, leading a pack mule and three unsaddled horses. Jory saw them coming and called a warning, and Merritt, Troop, and Laurie were there to greet them as they dismounted.

"Good to know you," Allgood said gruffly. "These're my boys, Houston and Zack."

"Ma'am," Houston said, looking at Laurie. He was the older of the two, maybe twenty-five.

Zack was about nineteen, tall and gangling, with some of the awkwardness of youth still on him. He grinned and ducked his head without speaking. From the banker's mention of them, Merritt had expected them to be younger. These two, he thought grimly, were about the right age to have had their share of the War.

"Glad you could come," Merritt said. "We weren't expecting you until a little later."

"I thought we'd want to talk things over." Allgood stroked his beard. "We rode over part of the trail to Fort Richardson coming here. Water hole's good, and we didn't see any Comanche sign. They mostly stay west of the river, these days. I remember —"

"Pa," Houston said gently, and Allgood shook his head.

"Oh, the horses. Mr. Whitlock, he said you might be a little short on horses, so we brought our own remuda. I reckon Zack could turn them into your corral, and maybe look to our mounts."

"Sure," Merritt said. "Billy can show you where everything is."

Allgood looked sharply at the big man. "Billy? Billy Troop. I couldn't mind your name." His long face broke into a smile, and he pumped Troop's hand. "We haven't seen you for ages."

"I been busy." Troop hunched his shoulders

162

and looked at the ground, then raised his head. "I'm working for the Yank now. I been teaching him about cows." He motioned to Zack and Houston. "Come on, I'll show you where to put your gear."

Watching them walk toward the barn, Allgood shook his head. After a moment, he looked at Merritt and Laurie. "That boy's really come along. Why, I remember when he first came back from the War—" Then he glanced again at Laurie and interrupted himself. "There I go again, storytelling. Ma'am, if you've got a cup of coffee, me and Mr. Merritt have a lot to talk about."

By suppertime, Merritt realized just what a good turn the banker had done him. Ben Allgood knew every inch of the country between Gilead and Fort Richardson, and he knew it with a cowman's eye for routes and water and good grazing. He also had a fund of stories about ranching and Indian fighting and the old days when Texas was a republic that held Jory spellbound — and Merritt as well. Merritt suspected he'd been replaced as Jory's hero, and he was amused at the twinge of jealousy that idea brought.

"You did right to come down here, Yank," Allgood said at supper. "This'll be good land, once it's settled and tamed. We'd have that done now, if we hadn't got mixed up in the War."

"Aw, Pa," Houston said. Merritt looked at the older man with interest.

"You sound like a Union man, Mr. Allgood."

"We should've listened to old Sam Houston," Allgood said. "He never wanted to throw in with the Confederacy. He figured we should go it alone if we left the Union."

"Aw, Pa," Houston said again. "We wanted to go and fight, Zack and me," he explained. "But Pa wouldn't have it."

"You didn't miss nothing much," Billy Troop growled from the foot of the table.

"I fought Santa Anna in '36 and again in '45," Allgood said firmly. "And I've fought Comanches 'most every year before and since. I wasn't intending to leave my woman and these boys' sisters to hold the place while we went hunting Yankees."

Houston evidently recognized the hopelessness of arguing. "This is a mighty good meal, ma'am," he said to Laurie. "I hope the food will be this good along the trail."

She smiled at him. "We've got the chuck wagon loaded, except for a few things. I think you'll get enough to eat."

"Houston's right, though," Allgood said. "I'd wish we could have you along to cook it for us. Now, I remember—"

Under cover of the story, Merritt saw Zack Allgood lean over to whisper something to Houston. Both laughed. Merritt frowned, unreasoning anger pulling at him. He knew well enough what they were thinking. If one of them said something out loud—

"Well, I guess we'd better turn in," Allgood said. He rose from the table, gathering up Zack and Houston with his eyes. "You go ahead, boys. I may just see if I can help with that chuck wagon a little."

"No, that's all right, Mr. Allgood," Laurie said. "I just have a few more things to do. You all will need rest, if you're going to start at daylight."

Allgood nodded. "Well, then, we'll just spread our bedrolls in that bunkhouse. Good night, ma'am, and thank you kindly."

Jory and Billy Troop were clearing the table. Merritt rose and went out with Allgood. The older men paused on the porch, looking up at the sky. The night was clear and warm, and the stars hung low and bright overhead.

"That's a mighty fine woman and boy in there," he said reflectively. "Her as good as a widow, too. You better not wait around too long, Yank. If Houston wasn't already spoke for, he'd probably be visiting here."

165

"I don't know what you mean," Merritt said stiffly. "And Clint was — is — my friend."

Allgood looked at him steadily in the dim light. "Beg pardon, then. I wasn't minded to talk out of turn." He stroked his long beard. "All the same, she's going to be up stocking that chuck wagon tonight. Was I you, I'd offer her a little help."

Humming to himself, he went across the yard and into the bunkhouse. Merritt took a step after him, swore, and went back into the kitchen. Troop was elbow-deep in a pan of soapy water, washing dishes while Jory dried.

"Don't you let Laurie see you," Troop said. He grimaced at Merritt. "She'll put you right to work."

"And I got to go to bed when I'm finished," Jory put in rebelliously. "It's not fair. I didn't get to hear near all of Mr. Allgood's stories."

Billy pulled his ugly face into a grin. "Nor you never would. I don't think that old man would ever run out of stories."

"You could tell me about the War," Jory said, looking hopefully up at Troop. "About the part you and Steve were in."

Billy put his head down for a moment. "Better not. I don't remember much that makes good telling." He wiped his hands and looked at Merritt. "You might as well turn in, Yank.

Me and Jory can finish up here, and I'll be sure his ma's getting along all right."

"All right. See you in the morning." Merritt turned to the door, stopped halfway through. "No, you go to bed when you're finished, Billy," he said. "I think I'll see if I can give Laurie a hand."

The old farm wagon was in the barn, newly fitted out with a crude wooden cupboard at the tailgate. Closed, it held pots, pans, tin plates, fire irons, and a variety of other cooking and eating gear that astonished Merritt. With the wide tailgate folded down, it made a sort of table where the cook could work. A big water barrel lashed to one side and a canvas possum belly underneath for holding firewood completed the change.

Merritt had fixed the whole thing up and provisioned it with the help of Sid Culver and the storekeeper. Looking at it now, he couldn't quite believe it was real.

"This is a lot of trouble to go to just to cover a hundred miles," he said.

Laurie, leaning over the tailgate to peer into the cupboard, glanced up at him. "You won't think so when you want a hot breakfast after the first cold night out," she said. "You need a big dishpan. Get the one from the house as soon as they're through with the dishes."

"Yes, ma'am."

"Did I sound like that? I'm sorry." She brushed her hair back from one eye. "Did you want something? I'm almost finished."

"Is there anything I can do to help?"

"Yes. Put those barrels of flour back up in the wagon bed. I don't know why we took them out." She frowned doubtfully at the two kegs. "That's a lot of flour. Do you think you'll need that much?"

"I have no idea. I told Mr. Evans where we were going, and took what he gave me."

Laurie laughed. "That's what I thought," she said. "I hope you're not doing the cooking."

Heaving up one of the flour barrels, Merritt set it carefully in the wagon. "I guess I am," he said. "The first day, at least. Mr. Allgood's going to take the point and I'll drive the wagon."

"Heaven help your stomachs," Laurie murmured. "There, that's fine."

She strained to lift the tailboard. Merritt came over to help her, shoving it up and latching it solidly in place.

"Thank you. That's heavier than I thought."

Laurie straightened, reaching up with both hands to sweep back her long hair. The movement brought her close to Merritt, her arm resting against his chest. Without moving away, she raised her face and looked directly at him for the first time since he'd come in. Her eyes lost their preoccupied look, were suddenly dark and serious. She looked tired, Merritt thought, thinner than he'd realized. Her hair smelled of flour and the hay of the barn and a warm, soft scent all her own.

"Tomorrow morning, then," she said flatly.

"You'll be all right," Merritt said. He knew that wasn't what she meant. "Billy and I will be back in less than ten days, and the marshal's promised to look in on you."

She didn't answer. Turning to him, she slid her hands along his back and drew herself against him, her head pressed to his chest. He couldn't see her face now, but her voice was low and clear.

"Steve, listen. I know what you've done for us, for Jory and me. At first, you were Clint's friend, and after that I was grateful, but now—" She let the words hang there for what seemed a long time, then said, "Steve, be careful. Come back safe."

Merritt raised his hands to her shoulders, his fingers closing so tightly he knew he must be hurting her. He ached to let go, to reach out to her, but something so deep inside that he couldn't even name it held him back. After a moment, she drew a long, shuddering breath and stepped away from him.

"Laurie, I'm sorry."

She shook her head, smiling. "No. I understand. But I had to tell you before you left." She picked up the lantern she'd been using and held it out to him. "We'd better say good night now. You have a long ride ahead of you tomorrow."

CHAPTER 11

The drive started off smoothly in the morning. Troop and the Allgoods hazed the cattle out of their pens and started them north while Laurie and Jory watched from the safety of the porch. A piebald old longhorn steer immediately took the lead. Disdainfully ignoring the riders, he stalked along the trail like a prophet, the other cows falling naturally in behind him.

"Look at that," Zack Allgood called. "Old Moses himself. He'll do our herding for us, do we just let him."

"You tend to those horses, boy," Houston answered. "Else you'll be doing your herding on foot."

As the cattle got themselves strung out and settled into a steady pace, Ben Allgood and Houston swung out to cover the flanks. Billy Troop rode drag, hazing along the stragglers, and Zack followed with their little remuda of horses. For a while, Merritt hung back to watch, but finally he gave the team its head.

He steered north along the road at first, then angled to the northeast, following the gentle curve of the river and avoiding Gilead and the more densely settled area around it. Gradually, the chuck wagon drew ahead of the herd. By midmorning, the only sign of the cattle Merritt could see was a low smudge of dust behind him.

It was a warm and drowsy day, its silence broken fitfully by the creaking of the wagon and the steady clop of hooves. Merritt had plenty of time to think — more time than he wanted, in fact. Laurie had been busy and cheerful before they left, preparing a big breakfast, warning them all to be careful, waving good-bye with Jory from the porch. She'd made no reference to their talk the night before, but Merritt knew her too well by now to believe she would forget it. Things were changing between them.

For the first time since he'd come to Gilead, Merritt realized how many lives were tied to his. Laurie, Jory, even Billy Troop, all were closer to him than anyone had been since — well, since sometime early in the War. He hadn't meant for that to happen. He'd come here on business, no other reason, and the townsfolk weren't likely to let him forget it.

A little after ten o'clock, Merritt drew up the wagon on a wooded knob above a long grassy valley. Taking a coil of rope from behind the seat, he strung it up between the stunted oaks to make a crude corral. Then he built a fire, put a pot of beans on to boil, and settled back to wait. Zack came in about an hour behind him, herding the spare horses into the corral.

"Better get ready, Cookie," the young cowhand called. "They're right behind me, and all hungry enough to eat the hair off a grizzly."

Troop and the others brought the herd up a little while later. Turning the cattle into the valley to graze, they rode up and dismounted by the wagon.

"Could be worse," Ben Allgood said, accepting the plate of beans and cold homemade bread that Merritt offered him. "They're looking right well."

Over a cup of coffee, Allgood sketched out a map of their route on the ground.

"There's a place we could stop about four hours ahead, with water and wood," he said. He raised his eyes to Merritt's. "Or maybe you'd rather make another hour or so. The river makes a curve up here" – he pointed – "and we could corral them in the loop for the night."

Merritt nodded. He'd seen this before in the Army – the way a good sergeant could run a company for the captain, without either ever letting on who was really in charge.

"Yes," he said. "I think we'd better do that."

Allgood raked the last of his food into the fire and straightened slowly. "This herding's almost too much for an old man." He motioned to the others. "All right, boys. Let's move."

While they changed horses, Merritt broke camp and loaded up the wagon. Before long, he was out ahead once more, watching over his shoulder as the herd plodded in his wake.

They camped that night at the spot Allgood had picked. Sitting before the fire after supper, the old cowman was cautiously optimistic about their little herd.

"We made better than twenty miles today, I figure – got those beeves away from everything they recognize. They won't stray far now." He paused, tested the wind with a moistened thumb. "We won't get along so fast from now on, but if the weather holds, we'll make Jim Bouldin's place in three, maybe four more days."

"Four more days and I'll be growed to that saddle," Zack put in. He was squatting loosely at his brother's side, hands hanging between his knees. "Ma always warned me never to get mixed up with cows."

Houston chuckled softly. "You wanted to be

174

a wrangler," he said. "Mr. Merritt's just giving you a little practice. Next year, maybe we'll trail to Kansas."

The younger man groaned, then heaved himself to his feet. "Best I go night-nurse those horses, then. Reckon we'll want 'em in the morning."

Merritt looked up at him in surprise. "Tonight? You'd better get some sleep. I can keep an eye on the herd."

"It's my job," Zack said quickly. Then he shrugged, and his irrepressible grin returned. "Don't worry, Yank. I'll sleep next winter."

"You turn in now, Mr. Merritt," Houston said. "You'll be first up in the morning. And I'll take the first shift on nighthawk, if nobody doesn't mind."

Billy Troop grunted. "Wake me up next. I don't sleep too good sometimes anyhow."

Old Ben Allgood smiled. "Now that's the thing about working with young men, Yank." He winked at Merritt. "They're always eager, and they let us old duffers snooze. Reckon I will."

Pulling his bedroll from the wagon, he spread it in a grassy spot near the fire and was asleep almost at once. Troop wasn't far behind. Merritt took longer, cleaning up the supper dishes and laying out some of the things he'd need in the morning. As he slipped off his boots, he heard the distant, mournful voice of Houston Allgood:

"A hundred months have flown, Lorena,
Since last I held that hand in mine
And felt thy pulse beat fast, Lorena,
Though mine beat faster far than thine."

It was a song Merritt knew well. He'd heard it from Rebel prisoners, and from the Rebel lines on quiet nights in camp. As so often before, it brought him a feeling he'd never been able to explain, a deep and aching loneliness even with Allgood and Troop snoring an arm's length away.

The next day was a copy of the first. Rising before dawn to wolf pancakes and coffee, they put a solid twenty miles behind them, stopping just short of the ford of the Clear Fork.
"We'll cross tomorrow, then push on toward old Fort Belknap," Allgood said. He hesitated, stroking his beard reflectively. Finally, he said, "Yank, maybe you'd like to let Zack drive the wagon tomorrow. You're going to make right smart of a cowman, but you ain't no kind of cook at all."
Laughing, Merritt agreed. He got a taste of

riding drag the next day. The going was slow at first, with the river crossing and a stretch of rough, broken country cut by shallow creeks. Toward evening, though, they regained the stage road. On the fourth day, Allgood promoted him to flanker and Billy Troop drove the chuck wagon. When they came into camp that evening, Troop was waiting with a meal of fried salt pork and gravy, pan biscuits, and a dutch-oven apple pie.

"We've had the wrong cookie all along," Zack vowed over his third slice of pie. "I didn't know you had all that talent, Billy."

Troop shrugged, trying not to look pleased. "Cooking ain't much," he growled. "You just take your time and think about what you're doing. Like fishing."

Later, when the others were asleep or out on their watches, Troop dropped down beside Merritt. Merritt had been staring into the fire, lost in thoughts that revolved around Clint and Laurie. He hadn't been getting anyplace, and he looked up at Troop gratefully.

"Hello, Billy. Can I help you clean up or anything?"

"I'm almost finished." Troop crossed his legs and put his big hands in his lap. "It ain't much."

They sat in silence for a minute or so. Finally, Merritt said, "Ben tells me we'll reach the

Bouldin place tomorrow. Fort Richardson's just a day beyond there. I guess the drive's about over."

"That's good," Troop said. "I'll be right glad to get back. I been—" He broke off, looking down at his hands. After a pause, he started again. "Hey, Yank, I been meaning to ask — what're you figuring to pay me?"

Caught by surprise, Merritt took a second to answer. Troop had never shown any interest in money — or even any awareness of it — before. Merritt turned to look closely at him, but the big man kept his head obstinately bowed over his hands.

"Well, I offered the job at thirty a month, back in the saloon that day. You've been worth a lot more, though. I couldn't have managed any of this without you. If you don't think that's enough—"

Now Troop did raise his eyes. "Thanks, Yank," he said. The firelight softened the lines of his scarred face, making him less ugly and more boyishly pleased. "Thirty's fine — for now, anyways."

Still puzzled, Merritt nodded toward the wagon. "I guess I owe you a little more than two months' wages. There's money in the cupboard, if you want to settle up."

"That's all right," Troop said. "I'd as leave

you kept it for me. I ain't too good at ciphering. I just been figuring that I might want it sometime."

"Whenever you say, Billy."

Troop lapsed back into silence, but Merritt had the feeling he wasn't quite through. He waited, chewing on a stem of the sweet grass that grew here. Sure enough, the big man finally cleared his throat.

"I been thinking." Troop looked off into the darkness where a hard edge of cloud was sliding in to cover the stars. His tone was strangely shy. "Being around folks again — Laurie, and that Jory's an awful good kid — well, I kind of thought I might want a place of my own sometime." He paused, then turned a belligerent scowl on Merritt. "I ain't said anything like that to anybody else. Most folks would think it's funny — old Simple Billy."

"I never called you that," Merritt said quietly. He'd once thought Troop was dangerous. Well, maybe he was. Laughing at him would be dangerous, all right. "And I don't see anything funny about it. I've been thinking that way myself."

Merritt glanced quickly at Troop. He hadn't meant to say that, hadn't even realized it was in his mind. The big man only nodded, though.

"I figured. But there's this girl in town — I

talked to her some, and she's been awful nice to me, even before I come to work for you. Maybe sometime—"

A burned-out log in the fire caved in, sending a shower of sparks up into the night sky. Troop jumped, then shook his head as if he was coming out of a dream.

"Hey — for a minute I thought that was —" He let the words trail off and got to his feet. "Guess I better saddle that old bay," he said, stretching his burly arms. "Houston'll be looking for me to relieve him."

The storm broke on them about three o'clock, with wind and driving wind and lightning that seemed to rip the whole sky apart. A shout from Ben Allgood routed them all from their bedrolls, and they spent the hours until dawn in the saddle, trying to keep the spooked herd milling under an endless cannonade of thunder. By the time the sky began to gray, the front had passed on. The rain settled down to a steady pounding, and Ben Allgood left Zack to watch the herd while he gathered the others near the chuck wagon.

"No point in trying to build a fire now," he said. He reached up to adjust his soggy hat. Outside his gleaming slicker, his beard hung limp as a drowned animal. "Let's get loaded and get 'em on the trail. We can pull up early for dinner, if this rain lets up. All right, Mr. Merritt?"

"All right," Merritt agreed. "I'll take the drag again, and Zack can handle the chuck wagon."

"No, you ride flank today. I'm about due a turn at drag," Allgood said. "Anyways, we ought to get to Bouldin's come supper. The boss better ride out in front."

The rain didn't let up. They made the best of a cold lunch and pressed on. The cows, hardly less tired than the men, plodded head-down behind Old Moses. Even on the muddy road, the chuck wagon couldn't keep up and slowly fell behind, Zack calling an ironic farewell from the wagon seat. Merritt, cold and bone-weary as he hadn't been since Appomattox, moved up and down the little herd's flank, not even the task of chasing strays lessening his discomfort.

At last, a tall gatepost loomed out of the rain ahead. Somewhat to his surprise, Merritt realized they'd been paralleling a fence for some time. He squinted up at the brand burned into the wood of the post – Circle B. They'd reached the Bouldin ranch.

Swearing to himself, he raced ahead and let the dun turn Old Moses. The steer gave him a disgusted look, but led the reluctant herd into a restless, milling circle. By that time, Troop and Allgood had caught up.

"Almost missed it," Merritt said. "Let's herd 'em in."

A man was waiting for them on the road, a wide, strapping man in a yellow slicker. He sat a gray horse with casual grace and ignored the rain completely as he offered a hand to Merritt.

"Jim Bouldin," he boomed. "We been expecting you boys. Turn those steers out to graze, and come up to the house. Reckon my cook's got supper waiting."

At the ranch house, Bouldin rapidly detailed two hands to tend to the horses, sent a couple more to look for Zack and the chuck wagon. Then he dismounted and led the way into the bunkhouse. It was a solid structure of chinked logs, and a fire burned brightly in the iron stove. The smell of fresh coffee filled the room.

"Help yourselves," Bouldin said. He stripped the dripping slicker off over his head and hung it on a peg. "Most of my boys are out now." He turned as Allgood came in. "Ben, good to see you again. I figured the Comanches had your hair by now."

Merritt, holding a cup of scalding coffee, took a moment to look at Bouldin for the first time. The rancher was younger than he'd expected, though his curly hair was shot with gray. His booming voice seemed to gather them all into a huge bear hug of goodwill. He turned again to shake hands with Houston and Billy Troop, and this time Merritt saw something awkward in the movement — a stiffness, as if one of Bouldin's legs didn't work quite right. Then the rancher waved toward a table at the far end of the room.

"You all get dried out. You can wash up out back if you need to. Soon's your last stray gets in with the wagon, we'll eat."

Later, he joined them at supper in the warm dimness of the bunkhouse. His wife did the serving, along with the plump Mexican girl who was also the cook.

"We don't get much company here," Bouldin said, winking at Merritt. "So my old woman listens to be sure I don't tell them something they shouldn't know."

"Only thing you don't know's when to keep quiet, Jim Bouldin," the woman said fondly. "More pie, Mr. Merritt?"

Merritt shook his head. "No, thanks, ma'am. I think that'll be enough."

"We're right glad to have you here," she said. "Jim's too bone-stubborn to deal with the Army himself, so we haven't had much hope of selling cows this year."

"Now, Martha." Bouldin shrugged his shoulders self-consciously. "I just don't quite feel right about that Yankee Army yet." He looked at the others. "Next year, it'll be better. Old Charlie Goodnight's trying to open a new trail up north. If he makes it, we'll all follow him. Right now, though, things are pretty tight. I don't deny your business was right welcome, Mr. Merritt."

"Even though I'm a Yankee?" Merritt asked curtly. There was silence for what seemed a long time, even Zack studying his plate intently. Then Bouldin cleared his throat.

"Sorry, Mr. Merritt. I'd plumb forgotten. I didn't mean anything against you. It's just—" He paused, forehead wrinkled in thought. "Well, you're a cowman now, same as us. Those blue-coat soldiers gave me this" — he rapped his knuckles on his right thigh with a solid, wooden sound — "and that takes some getting used to."

"I'm sorry," Merritt said.

Bouldin grinned. "I'm not. I'm home, safe with my woman. There's lots of folks got worse."

"Yeah," Billy Troop said unexpectedly. He shoved back his chair and got up. "It don't all show, neither. I think I'll turn in."

In the silence that followed this time, everybody looked at Merritt. Again, it was Jim Bouldin who broke the tension.

"I expect Martha's right, though," he said. "We'd best put all that behind us." He rose, pivoting on the stiff right leg, and gestured toward the door. "If you all are through, I have a brand-new Appaloosa colt out in the barn you ought to see. Be just right for a youngster, I'd say."

CHAPTER 12

Except for the swift-flowing green water of Lost Creek and the backdrop of hills with their thick groves of oak, Fort Richardson might have been any frontier post Merritt had ever seen. They might differ in details of construction, but the forts were all basically the same — Lancaster, deep in the Devil's River country, and Phantom Hill, and Mason, where Lee had commanded before the War, and all the rest. They shared an air of impermanence, of being forever half-finished. Wood and canvas hackadales — half shanty, half tent — stood among solid frame buildings, and new stone walls rose near cedar-shake cabins abandoned and falling down.

Fort Richardson was no exception. From where Merritt stood at the corner of the quartermaster's corral, he could watch work parties swarming over the skeleton of the hospital. Barracks and officers' quarters faced each other across a bleak parade ground, and horses pawed restlessly in the cavalry corrals close by. The whole scene, with its familiar smells and sounds and the hurrying blue figures everywhere, gave Merritt an almost overwhelming feeling of being back in the Old Army, as if the War and the time between had never happened.

Evidently, it struck Billy Troop differently. As soon as the cattle were safely in the corral, the big man edged over to Merritt.

"If it's all the same to you, Yank, I reckon I'll go into town," he growled. He scuffed his boots in the dust and stared at the ground. "Being around this many bluebelly soldiers makes me right uneasy."

"Sure, Billy, but stay out of trouble over there. I'd better wait until the clerk's through tallying the cattle."

"Oh, nobody gives me trouble." Troop flexed his big shoulders and laughed. His blue eyes were clear. "Anyway, I figured I'd stick with Ben and the boys. They're going over soon's they get the spare horses stabled. The sutler said we could leave them and the wagon here."

Merritt dug in his pocket, found a half eagle. "Good." He slipped the money into Troop's hand. "Buy the Allgoods a drink and a steak for me. I'll meet you when I can."

"Be careful," Troop advised in turn. "You watch them Yankees, or they'll cheat you blind.

Can't trust a one of them."

He walked away, whistling tunelessly. Merritt frowned after him, then turned as a bored-looking commissary clerk strode up to the corral. The soldier climbed onto the top rail and perched there, holding a pencil and notebook.

"All right, let's put them through the chute." He gestured impatiently to a couple of troopers standing by the fence. "Get that gate open. Let's get this over with."

The corral was divided into two parts, connected by a narrow chute. Cattle penned in one side could be hazed one at a time into the other. One of the privates slipped down into the unoccupied side of the enclosure and swung back the gate of the chute, then scurried back as a curious longhorn poked his head in to investigate. With many shouted instructions and much running about, the three troopers started their count.

Merritt stood by silently, checking the tally and thinking how easy the job would be for a couple of men on horseback. They had barely started when an officer approached from the direction of the barracks. Seeing Merritt, he broke into a run.

"Steve! Steve Merritt! By thunder, it is you! I wouldn't have believed it."

Merritt turned to meet a warm handshake

and an eager pounding on his back. "You remember me? George Summers. Why it must be—"

"—three years," Merritt finished. "Nearer four. It was while you were on Sedgwick's staff, just before the Wilderness."

"That's right." Summers nodded eagerly. "I went west in the reorganization — wound up here in Texas before the end, in fact, and I've been here ever since."

"It seems to agree with you," Merritt said with a smile.

At first glance, he might not have recognized the lean, intense staff captain he'd known from the Army of the Potomac. Summers had come from the Old Army, just as Merritt had. That had given them a common bond and, though they hadn't exactly been friends, they'd spent a good deal of time together. Then Summers had been transferred and "Uncle John" Sedgwick had caught a sniper's bullet at Spotsylvania, and Merritt went into the hell of Cold Harbor and Petersburg.

Summers wore a major's leaves now, but the change went deeper than that. His once-thin face had filled out, the cheeks a little puffy and flushed from the sun, and a walrus moustache shadowed his mouth. He'd put on weight, too, a pleasant chubbiness that showed he wasn't spending too much time riding patrols.

Reading Merritt's thoughts, Summers laughed and patted his stomach complacently.

"That's what the quartermaster corps will do for you." He gestured at the bawling steers. "I spend most of my time doing this sort of thing now. I'm one of those coffee coolers we used to damn."

"That seems like a long time ago."

"A different world." For a moment, the major looked much more like the man Merritt had known. Then he laughed and slapped Merritt on the back again. "So you're down by Phantom Hill now, eh? Have you had any trouble there?"

"What kind of trouble?"

"Oh, you know. These ex-Rebs don't think too much of Union men moving in." The officer's face hardened a little. "They'll be seeing more of it, though. A lot of them are going to be sorry they got mixed up in the rebellion."

"A lot of them already are," Merritt murmured. Aloud, he said, "There's been some friction." Without thinking, he dropped a hand to touch the butt of his Navy Colt. "Nothing I can't handle."

"Well, if there's anything you need, just let me know. We need more of your kind in Texas." Summers laughed suddenly and waved a hand toward officers' row. "Hey, I'm forgetting my manners. Leave the count to my clerk and come on over to my quarters. We'll have a drink and trade lies."

"You were right to get out, Steve," Summers was saying. He stared out the window at the sun-drenched parade ground. "The Army's mostly a police force now. We protect the carpetbag government from the citizens and the citizens from the Comanches, and none of them appreciate us. Damned if I don't think I like the Comanches best. At least they'll give you a stand-up fight."

Merritt said nothing. He sat at a field desk in the dark frame bungalow, a tumbler of whiskey untouched at his elbow. In the hour since they'd come in from the corrals, Summers had downed three similar shots, and Merritt was beginning to realize not all the flush in the major's pink cheeks came from the sun.

"It'll get better, though. We're moving to a new line of forts on the border of Comanche country. Then we'll see some real action." He waved vaguely toward the southwest. "Got one started on the Clear Fork, about twenty miles from your place. We'll be building next month. Can you supply us beef?"

"Sure," Merritt said. "I ought to tell you,

though, there are other ranchers around there who can do it as well as I can."

Summers rose and got himself a fresh drink. The neck of the bottle chattered against the glass. "Rebs," he said thickly. "We have orders to give preference to loyal men. Loyal!" His tone made the word sound like a curse. "Most of the loyal men here came in behind the troops — sharpers and highbinders out for a fast profit. So, maybe you've got a contract. I'll see."

"Thanks," Merritt said. "I appreciate that." He rose, sliding his chair back into place. "Your clerk should be through by now," he reminded Summers. "I'd better get over to town and pay off my hands."

"Oh?" The major looked at him with vague disappointment. "Come over to the commissary, then, and I'll write you a draft. Hate to see you go — it's good to talk to somebody that remembers."

He straightened. "Hey, did I tell you we fought close to Phantom Hill, right at the end — oh, June of '65, I guess. Did I tell you?"

"No." Merritt leaned forward, suddenly interested. "I'd heard you were in Kansas then. What happened?"

Summers thumped his fist on the desk. "Rebels," he said huskily. "Texas troops —

irregulars. Shot up a supply depot right on the Kansas border, and we were ordered to get them. Chased them all the way down here. We finally captured a few — rear guard, I guess — but the Comanches got the rest. Good joke on them."

"And that was at Phantom Hill?"

"Just a few miles off. They must've known the country. Seemed like they were making right for it."

Merritt frowned. "Why would they do that? There's nothing there but chimneys and foundations. They must have been headed somewhere else."

"Crazy," Summers said. "Crazy Rebs." Swaying a little, he stared owlishly at Merritt. "Oh, yeah. Going for your draft. Come on." At the door, he stopped and turned to put a hand on Merritt's arm. "Remember, you need anything, just let me know. Us old war-horses, we gotta stick together."

"Thanks, George," Merritt said. "I'll remember that. Let's get that draft now, all right?"

A narrow wooden bridge spanned the creek down behind the cavalry stables. Merritt walked across it, pausing in the middle to look into the rushing water. He knew Billy and the Allgoods had taken their horses — he would've bet that none of the Allgood clan would walk more than fifty feet by choice — but Merritt had seen enough of horses for the balance of this trip.

The approach to the bridge opened directly into the main street of the town, such as it was. A narrow track, muddy and churned by innumerable hooves, it was lined on either side by tents and picket cabins. Some bore crude signs offering whiskey or gambling, while others were unmarked. A pretty, dark-haired girl came to the doorway of one of these as Merritt passed.

"Hey, cowboy, come in and visit." She tossed her head toward the buildings farther up the street. "They'll just cheat you on up the line."

She was young, Merritt saw, barely out of her teens. She wore a loose white blouse, cut low in front, and her smile was brightly mercenary. Beneath her heavy makeup, she looked tired.

"Sorry. I'm looking for some friends."

"I'll be your friend."

He shook his head and walked on, hearing the girl's curse behind him. The horses were tied in front of a big wagon-sheet tent at the end of the street. Merritt ducked inside. The Allgoods and Billy Troop were seated around a rough trestle table in one corner. Zack Allgood saw Merritt and waved him over.

"Holler at that lady at the stove, Yank, and she'll bring your steak. We're just about to finish up."

"Would've been finished a sight sooner, if Zack hadn't found the pie," Houston said. He eased down a bit on the wooden bench. "Have a seat, Mr. Merritt."

"Thanks. How's the food?"

The four men looked at each other. "Well," Houston said, "we don't have to fix it ourselves. That's something. And Zack hasn't found fault with the pie."

"Right." Zack looked up as the woman who ran the place bustled over to serve Merritt steak, beans, and coffee. "I'll have another piece of that when you get the chance, ma'am."

"I hope you have a big ranch, Mr. Allgood," Merritt said. "Otherwise you can never afford to feed that kid."

Ben Allgood smiled absently. "It's been a good little drive," he said. "Kind of sorry we're finished up." He tugged thoughtfully at his beard. "Maybe we ought to stay together another night. We could take the wagon and camp a ways out on the prairie, and the boys and me could ride along a piece with you tomorrow."

Merritt saw Zack wink at Houston. The boy

pushed back his empty plate and cleared his throat.

"Ah, Pa, I wonder if I could meet you all out there a little later. To tell the truth, I kind of have a hankering to look around town some."

"This place is a den of vice and iniquity," Ben Allgood said sternly. "You're wanting to waste your pay on cards and women – don't try to tell me different."

"No, Pa." Zack sounded contrite. Then he said, "Pa? You remember telling us about when you went to the Mexican War, and that place down in Matamoros?"

For a moment, Merritt thought Ben Allgood was going to burst a blood vessel. The rancher's face flushed deep red, but instead of bursting out in anger, he suddenly began to laugh.

"I tell you, Yank," he said. "It's a terrible thing when a man gets caught by his own lies." He glared at Houston. "I suppose you want to squander your substance, too."

"Well – I thought I might ought to stay around and see Zack keeps out of trouble."

"Umm." Allgood considered briefly. "Yank, give these boys a five-dollar note. They should be able to do all the sightseeing they'll need on that. I believe I'll just hold the rest of their pay."

Laughing, Merritt passed the money across.

Then he glanced at Troop, who'd been sitting quietly by, lost in some thought of his own.

"Billy? Do you want to stay, too?"

Troop blinked and raised his head. "What? Oh, no, Yank. I'll wait around 'til you're through eating, then ride out with you and Mr. Allgood." He looked down at the tabletop. "I'll wait my turn 'til we get back home."

The three of them made camp along the stage road a few miles south of the fort. Merritt, free for the first time in days from worry about the herd, was surprised to find how tired he was. Even so, he sat up late into the night with Troop and Ben Allgood, watching the flames from their lonely fire and listening to the old rancher's limitless fund of stories. He awoke again when Zack and Houston stumbled in not long before dawn. They tended their horses and spread their bedrolls, talking and laughing with muffled hilarity until their pa grumbled them to silence. Feeling himself a part of them all, Merritt rolled onto his back and looked up with a quiet happiness into the vaulted arch of the night sky until he fell asleep.

Morning came in clear and hot, finding them already on the road. Troop drove the chuck wagon while Zack and Houston, both unusually quiet, kept the remuda together. Today, there was traffic on the road — the mail coach beginning its long desert passage to El Paso, a column of troopers inbound for Fort Richardson, half a dozen cowhands headed for town and a spree.

Early that afternoon, they came again to the ruins of old Fort Belknap on the Salt Fork of the Brazos. Another trail intersected the main road there, and Ben Allgood reined in his horse at the crossing.

"I reckon we'd best leave you, Yank. We can cut off nigh twenty miles to our place by taking this way."

"Well, it's been a pleasure, Mr. Allgood. Do you have enough supplies to see you through?"

The rancher patted his saddlebags. "Oh, we'll manage," he said. "Houston, tie off Billy's horse to the wagon, and bring ours along."

Troop drove up with the wagon and Zack and Houston came over to shake hands all around. Houston merely smiled his quiet smile and nodded, but Zack said, "Sure enjoyed it, Yank." He winked impishly. " 'Specially last night. Did you see that black-haired gal who lived down by the bridge?"

"Zack!" Ben Allgood's tone was sharp, but he was smiling, too. He stuck out his hand to Merritt. "Have a good trip back, Yank. And don't forget we're neighbors. If there's anything we can do—"

"If I have more work like this, I'll let you know," Merritt said. "Banker Whitlock can bring you word."

Allgood's smile tightened a little. "Much obliged," he said shortly. "Good luck to you, Yank. Adios, Billy."

He reined around and started up the trail, the boys bringing the horses up in a loose bunch behind him. Merritt watched them until a clump of scrub oak hid them from sight, then turned to look squarely into Billy Troop's accusing eyes.

"I guess—" Merritt began, then saw Troop's expression. "What's the matter, Billy?"

"Yank, that's the best old man in the world, and just trying to be friends with you. Why'd you go and treat him that way?"

"I don't know what you mean," Merritt said, though deep down, he did. "This drive helped them with the banker. They were just doing it for the money. There wasn't anything else."

Troop snorted. "I guess I ain't your friend, neither, then," he said. "Yank, you sure make it hard for folks to like you, sometimes."

He started to whip up the team, but Merritt, suddenly angry, leaned over and caught his arm.

"Listen, Billy. Since I came here, I've been

beaten up, shot at, and a bunch of my neighbors made a good try at lynching me. Maybe you figure that's just being friendly, but I don't think I fit in with this bunch of—"

Merritt stopped abruptly. "—Rebs," he'd meant to finish. He remembered his reaction to the major's tirade the day before. Summers was still fighting the War, he'd thought – but maybe Summers wasn't the only one.

Troop pulled his arm away. For a moment, his eyes dulled with the ugly, animal look they'd worn the first time Merritt had seen him. Then the big man shook himself and sighed.

"Yank," he said in a slow, patient voice, "you don't want to fit in – not here or anyplace. Every time somebody offers you a hand, you got to slap it away. Likely you'd do the same to me, 'cept you know I'm crazy. But the way you been doing Laurie—"

The big man snapped his mouth shut abruptly. Before Merritt could even begin to answer, Troop shook the lines and started the team moving. Merritt sat still, holding the dun in check, staring after the wagon. Looking at it honestly, he knew Troop was right. People had come out to meet him halfway – Jory, the marshal, Tom Drake, Ben Allgood and his sons, even Major Summers. And Laurie. Each time, he'd been the one to draw back. He'd been drawing back for a long time, since sometime in the War.

The memory came to him clear and sharp — Cedar Creek, 1864, Sheridan's little army victorious and relaxing in camp. Himself struggling out of his bunk before dawn to strap on revolver and sword belt. "I'd better get along. The old man wanted me to inspect the defenses along the creek. He thinks First Corps is getting careless." And Wade saying, "You were up most of the night, Steve. Let me take it — what are friends for?"

Then the yell and Early's scarecrow troops bursting out of the woods on the right flank, First Corps smashed and the rest driven back in such a near rout that it took Sheridan himself to get it untangled and pull out a victory. A lot of good men had died that day. One of them was Major Obed Wade, Merritt's friend — the last friend he'd had.

It was easy for Troop to talk, Merritt thought bitterly. He hadn't been through what Merritt had, hadn't made friends just to see them killed. He didn't know—

That thought died as soon as he'd shaped it. Troop did know. He'd been in the same war, in the same places, but on the other side. And something there had hurt him so much that he was only now starting to get over it.

"We ought to stick together, Yank," Troop had said once. "We're the same kind of folks." Now, Merritt suddenly realized what the big man had meant. They'd both been hit the same way. Troop had gone inside his mind where he couldn't be reached, while Merritt had turned away from people, afraid ever to let them get close again. That was the only difference between them – and now, Billy was slowly getting well.

Merritt didn't know how long he sat there, but the chuck wagon was far down the trail by the time he turned the dun and spurred after it. He fell in beside the wagon and rode in silence for a way, then looked at Troop. The big man was hunched on the wagon box, his eyes stubbornly on the road ahead.

"Billy?" Merritt said. "How far do you suppose it is over to Bouldin's place?"

Troop frowned at him in surprise. "Oh, not so very far if we double back to the other trail. Why?"

"I think we ought to ride by there," Merritt said. "I've been thinking about that Appaloosa colt. Bouldin was right – that would be a perfect horse for a youngster."

CHAPTER 13

It was late in the morning when Troop and Merritt rode back into the yard of the LJ. The sun was high and hot, and a mockingbird was screaming from somewhere down toward the river. The sharp fragrance of burning cedar hung in the still air. Merritt, beside Billy on the wagon box, stood up and cupped his hands to his mouth.

"Hello! Where is everybody?"

From down by the barn came a frantic cackling of chickens, then a whoop from Jory. The boy came tearing around the corner of the stock pens and landed in Troop's lap with what seemed a single leap.

"Billy! Steve! We thought you'd come yesterday, and then Ma said it wouldn't probably be for another couple of days, so we weren't looking for you. Did you sell the cows? Did you see any Indians? Did you talk to the Yankee soldiers? Did you bring me anything?"

"Whoa, there." Billy Troop lifted him by one

arm and the seat of the pants and set him carefully on the wagon seat. "You hold these lines. And just ask one question at a time. You know I don't think too fast."

"Hello, Jory," Merritt said. "Where's your mother?"

"Oh, she's out back—"

"Here I am, Steve."

Laurie had come out on the porch of the cabin. She came down the steps toward the wagon, hugging herself with her arms as if to hide. She wore a shapeless calico dress, and her long hair was tucked up underneath a white kerchief. She put her hands up to straighten it, then lowered them helplessly to her sides.

"I thought you'd come yesterday, so I put off doing the washing and made myself all pretty, and today I was just heating up the kettles. Men!" She raised her hands again, then clasped them together with a little gesture of frustration. "Oh, but I'm thankful to see you, though. We were worried about you — the two of you — on the trail."

Merritt stepped down from the wagon, and she came quickly to him, taking his arm. "I'm glad you're back," she said, this time directly to him.

"Me, too. It went just fine. Was everything all right here?"

A hint of worry came and went in her eyes, and then she nodded. "Yes," she said, with a quick glance at Jory. "We stayed pretty close to home."

"Reckon we would've been home a day early, but for the Yank," Billy Troop put in. "He had to stop at every general store anyways near our trail, buying pretties." He winked ponderously at Merritt. "Seems we did bring something for old Jory. Where'd you put it, Yank?"

Merritt patted his pockets while Jory watched anxiously. Finding nothing, he frowned, then snapped his fingers.

"I know, Billy. I tied it behind the wagon, remember?"

"Aw." Jory's look was openly unbelieving, but he scrambled off the wagon seat fast enough and scampered around to the back. There was a silence, and then he yelled, "Ma, come quick! Look!"

Laurie and Merritt followed more slowly. The horses were neck-roped together to trail behind the wagon, and Merritt had tied the Appaloosa colt nearest the tailboard where he wasn't easily visible from in front. Jory was standing beside him, staring as if he expected him to disappear.

"Steve — did you really — is he mine? Did you mean it?"

"Sure did, Jory," Merritt said, over Laurie's stifled protest. "Billy and I decided you were about ready for your own horse. Jim Bouldin says he's broken to saddle, but he may need a little while to get used to you."

"Reckon we could get started on that right now," Billy Troop said. He'd come around the far side of the wagon, and now stood grinning at Jory. "You and me could water these animals and turn 'em into the pens. Likely you could start getting to know him then."

"Oh, boy! Ma, I'll get some carrots from the cellar for him. That'll be all right, won't it?"

He fumbled with the knot, finally got it loose, and led the horses toward the barn. Troop went around to unhitch the team, then followed him. When they had gone, Laurie pulled a little bit away from Merritt and looked up at him, half angrily.

"Steve, you had no business doing that."

"You don't mind his having the colt, do you? It's gentle enough."

"No, it isn't that. But you shouldn't have been the one to buy it. You've done so much for us already, that—"

He interrupted firmly. "It's an investment. I figure Jory's going to be our top hand one day. Strictly business." He turned to rummage in the wagon bed, then handed Laurie a bulky parcel wrapped in paper. "Here, I brought something for you, too."

"Steve — what?" Laurie's eyes still held a questioning look. She tore into the heavy wrappings, revealing a length of creamy white lace. "Steve — oh! It's the curtains!"

"Nottingham lace, the storekeeper said. The last set he had." Merritt shrugged. "If you don't like them, I can always hang them in the bunkhouse. Billy would like that."

"Oh, Steve, you idiot. Thank you."

Impulsively, she reached up with her free arm and caught Merritt, standing on tiptoe to give him a quick kiss on the mouth. At least, she'd meant it to be quick. There was nothing impulsive about Merritt's reaction. He gathered her, curtains and all, into his arms and returned the kiss thoroughly.

When he released her, she stayed there, staring up at him in wide-eyed surprise. Before she could speak, Jory came running from the house, trailing a bunch of carrots behind him.

"He likes me," the boy called. "I'm going to call him Traveler — Billy says that was General Lee's horse. Come and look, Ma."

"In a minute, Jory." She stepped back quickly, wonder still showing in her eyes as she looked at Merritt. "I'd better — Jory, don't bother Steve and Billy right now. Let them get cleaned up. I need to fix us some lunch."

"Aw, Ma."

Merritt turned, scooping the boy up. "Your ma's right. Come on. You can give those carrots to your horse, then help us unload. If you're going to be a top hand, you'd better get to work."

When Merritt emerged from the bunkhouse later, shaved and with most of the accumulated trail dust scrubbed away, Laurie had thrown together a hasty lunch. She'd also found time to brush out her hair and change into a blue housedress that he hadn't seen before. She ate little, but listened intently as Merritt, with many interruptions from Billy Troop, told the story of their drive. Jory was torn between listening and running out every couple of minutes to Traveler's pen.

"Jory's going to have all the hair petted off that colt by morning," Billy Troop chuckled. "That was a right good thought, Yank."

"The curtains weren't a bad idea, either," Merritt answered, and Laurie looked down at the table, her cheeks showing pink.

Troop excused himself before dessert and went outside. When Merritt and Laurie stepped out onto the porch a few minutes later, the big man was coming from the barn, leading the saddled bay. He stopped at the foot of the steps, looking up at Merritt.

"Hey, Yank, you think our cows can wait another day? I thought I might ride into town for a spell and — go by the store."

"Well, Jory and I can take care of the chuck wagon and get everything put away," Merritt said. "I guess you have a day off coming, anyway. Do you need some money?"

"Well, I know I asked you to hold my pay, but —"

Merritt grinned. "Sure, Billy." He fished in his pocket, came up with a mixture of bills and silver. "This is all I have on me right now. Will that do?"

"That's good." Troop pocketed the money without looking at it. He swung onto the bay, then hesitated, his eyes on the ground. "Uh — Yank, if I run late, I reckon I won't ride back in the dark. Somebody in town'll probably put me up."

Merritt nodded gravely. "All right, Billy. Take care."

"Yeah. Thanks."

He reined the bay around and rode off without looking back. Laurie watched him curiously.

"Now, why would he want to go to the store today, after the ride you've had? And why wouldn't he come back?"

"No reason," Merritt said. "I think he just wants to show his old friends that he's a man."

Before dark, Merritt pried Jory away from the colt long enough to get a few chores done. Then he let the boy go while he finished unloading the chuck wagon by the light of a lantern. He was just putting away the last of the gear when Laurie came through the door of the barn.

"Steve? I was looking for Jory. It's his bedtime."

Merritt turned quickly. "Didn't he go back to the house? I told him—" He stopped, a grin spreading over his face. "I'll bet I know. Come on."

The lantern's flickering light showed Jory curled in a ball by the corner of Traveler's pen. He was sound asleep. The colt stood near him, velvet nose lowered to sniff curiously at an outstretched hand. Merritt handed the light to Laurie and stooped to pick the boy up. Jory stirred, then opened his eyes.

"Hi, Steve. Is it morning?"

"Not yet. Let's go in."

Merritt carried the boy into the cabin, waited while Laurie listened to his sleepy prayers and tucked him into bed. When she came down the ladder from the loft, she was smiling.

"He went to sleep telling me he wanted to

stay up and play with Traveler," she said. "Thank you, Steve. I haven't seen him so happy since — not for months." She turned away suddenly, walking to the cabin's front door. "There's coffee on the stove. Would you like some?"

"No." Merritt came up behind her and put his hands on her shoulders. She turned softly to him. "Laurie, there's something — something I've been thinking about ever since Billy and I started back."

"So long?" Her tone was teasing, but her eyes were wide and attentive. "It must be important."

"It is to me."

Laurie was close against him, her face turned up to his. He started to speak, then bent instead and found her lips. For an instant, she held back — surprise, denial, he couldn't tell. Then her arms slid around his neck and her body seemed to flow into his. After a long time, she broke away and pressed her face against his chest.

"You've changed," she whispered.

"Yes," Merritt said. He remembered when Elizabeth had said those same words to him. Then he had been drawing away from her, from people, into himself. Now it was different. "Laurie," he said into her hair, "I hadn't meant it to be like this. The ranch, Clint — I don't know what we'll do. But I need you, Laurie."

Her shoulders trembled in a long sigh. "Oh, Steve." Now she looked at him, tears shining in her eyes. "That's hard for you, I know — needing somebody."

"It was. Now it'll be better. It's something that happened—"

She stopped him with a kiss. "Not now," she said, her mouth still against his. "I want you to tell me, but not now. I've waited for you such a long time."

Merritt awakened late. The moon was low in the west and almost too bright to look at. Its cold light streamed through the bunkhouse window, throwing everything into sharp black and white. Turning his head a little, Merritt could see Laurie's face, younger and less decided than usual, the lips slightly parted in sleep. Her body was warm beneath the rough blanket that covered them, the gentle rise of her breast soft against his chest.

She'd gone to sleep on his shoulder, and his arm was cramped and numb from lack of circulation. He shifted to ease it, trying not to wake her, but she stirred and yawned.

"Steve," she murmured. She sounded drowsy,

but her eyes showed no uncertainty or confusion. Merritt liked that. "It's late. I have to go in."

He bent and kissed her half-open mouth. "No. Stay with me."

"Jory's in the cabin," she said practically. "I have to be there if he wakes up and calls. I shouldn't have stayed this long."

"Sorry you did?"

He'd meant to ask that lightly, but it didn't quite come out that way. Laurie raised herself on one elbow. She touched Merritt's face with her fingertips, looking steadily into his eyes.

"In a way I am. We shouldn't be here, like this. Now we're just like Frank Harmon thought we were."

"No," Merritt said softly. "You said you'd waited a long time, Laurie. So had I, but that's not why we're here. There's more to it."

She closed her eyes. "I know."

Abruptly, she sat up and let the blanket fall away. She reached for her clothing, dressing quickly and without shyness. "We'll have to work it out," she said.

"Sure. But don't worry."

"I'm not worried."

He rose and went to the door with her, padding barefoot across the cold earthen floor. They kissed for a moment, and then she stepped out into the moonlight.

"Good night, Laurie."

"Good night." She paused, a playful smile tugging at her mouth. "You'd better get back to bed," she said. "You'll catch your death."

She turned and ran swiftly across the yard to the cabin. Merritt watched until she was safely inside, then closed the door and went back to his empty bunk. To his surprise, he slept.

When Merritt came into the cabin the next morning, Laurie, humming softly, was fitting the lace curtains to the front window. She looked up and called a muffled greeting through a mouthful of pins. Giving the curtains a last critical look, she stepped back and started returning the pins to a red lacquered box.

"Those can be altered to fit just fine," she said. "There's coffee on the stove. Billy hasn't come back yet, and Jory's still asleep." She smiled at Merritt, mischief in her eyes. "You slept late this morning, yourself."

Merritt took a cup from the shelf and poured coffee. "I've been awake for quite a while," he said. "I was thinking about — well, about last night."

"Oh," Laurie said in a different tone. She turned her back and busied herself with the curtains again. "It doesn't give me any hold on you, Steve, if that's what you're thinking. You're still free, if you want to be."

He laughed sharply. "I've been free, thanks. That's not it." He put the cup down and leaned back against the counter. "Now we have another problem. I have to find Clint."

Laurie turned, her eyes suddenly wide and frightened. "Steve, no," she said. "Leave it to the marshal." She came to him, sliding her arms around his waist. "Clint's gone. I know that now. I've lost him – and I don't want the same thing to happen to you."

Reluctantly, Merritt shook his head. "Laurie, I can't leave it. You're still his wife, and I'm still his friend – nothing's changed that. One way or the other, we have to know what happened. Don't you see that?"

"Yes." Her voice was very soft. "And – if he's alive? If he comes back?"

"We'll handle it when it happens. But we have to know."

"Yes," she repeated. "We have to know." She rubbed her head against his shoulder and he reached up to stroke her hair. "Steve? The marshal's looked for months. What can we do?"

"I may know of a way," Merritt said. "But don't worry about it now. I think Jory's awake."

They both looked toward the loft. There were muffled sounds, then the boy's sleepy voice:

"Ma? Is breakfast ready?"

"In a minute, sweetheart." She stepped away from Merritt, rubbing a hand across her eyes. "All right. Breakfast in a few minutes. Then you can get started."

She turned briskly toward the stove. Merritt hesitated, then said, "Laurie?"

"Yes?"

"Laurie, about last night – I don't promise it won't happen again."

Now she laughed, and the familiar playful smile swept away for the moment the lines of worry around her mouth.

"That's what I was going to tell you," she said.

CHAPTER 14

"Well, good morning, Mr. Merritt." The marshal's sad smile welcomed Merritt into the office. "Haven't seen you for a spell. I expect you're just here to thank me for running a nice, quiet town."

Merritt pulled a chair up close to the marshal's desk and sat down. Thinking about it ahead of time, he'd decided he wasn't the man to outsmart Bell. He'd tackle him head on, and see what happened.

"I need a description of Mary Beth Rankin, Marshal," he said now. "The same one you sent out with the circular on Clint. I think I can help you find her."

Bell leaned back in his chair and squinted thoughtfully at Merritt. "I can't quite recall asking for any help," he said. "Seems like I'd suggested you stay out of manhunting."

"Sorry, Marshal," Merritt said. "I've waited about as long as I can. I intend to find out what's happened to Clint, with or without your help."

The lawman raised his eyebrows, but let Merritt's words pass. "Miz Davidson doesn't believe Mary Beth's leaving had anything to do with Clint," he reminded Merritt. "You think different?"

"Sure I do. So do you. Two people disappearing from Gilead the same night can't be a coincidence. If the girl's alive, the chances are she knows where Clint is."

"Maybe," Bell conceded. He thought for a moment. "Maybe," he repeated, more strongly. "Now, how do you propose—?"

He broke off at a sound from the back of the office. The door leading back to the cells swung open, and Frank Harmon came through.

"I'm finished in back, Marshal," Frank began. "I thought—" Then he caught sight of Merritt and stopped, his face hardening into a scowl. "Well, the Army of the Potomac. I figured somebody had killed you by now."

"You want the job?"

Merritt came smoothly to his feet and turned to face the deputy's challenging stare. Then, abruptly, he changed his mind and relaxed. If he was going to try getting along with these people, Frank might be a pretty good place to start.

"Frank, listen," he said. "I'm planning to be here a long time. I'd like to settle our differences so we don't square off to fight every time we see each other. How about it, Texas Mounted Rifles?"

The deputy had listened without changing his expression, but at the last words, something new – surprise, Merritt thought, though it looked almost like fear – came into his eyes. Before Merritt had time to puzzle over that, Bell spoke up.

"Sounds like a fair offer, Frank. What do you say?"

The deputy looked at Merritt, and his face was closed again. "The only way this Yank can settle with me is to go back where he came from." He strode to the front door. "I'll take my round now, Marshal. Maybe the office will be cleaner when I come back."

After Frank had gone, Bell sat in brooding silence. Merritt sank back into the chair, slowly unclenching balled fists, and waited for the marshal to speak.

"I don't know," Bell said, half to himself. "That boy –" He shook his head and fell silent again.

"It's partly my fault, Marshal," Merritt said. "I had another run-in with Frank out at the Rankin place not long ago. I was there asking questions, and I guess he was, too. Maybe that was what –"

"Wait a minute." Bell suddenly focused on Merritt again. "Frank? When was that?"

"Oh, a month or so back, maybe. The same day I bought the stock from Tom Drake. You said you'd be looking for something new on Clint, so I figured that was why he was there."

"Oh, yeah. Yeah." The marshal frowned, then said, "Never mind. You were telling me about the girl. I don't see how you figure to find her, when none of the lawmen around here have had any luck."

"Maybe she's someplace there isn't any law. Around one of the forts, say."

Bell whistled. "Son, those scab towns are tough as a hickory stump. You go prowling around them, somebody'll just about bury you."

"That's been tried," Merritt said. He leaned forward. "Soldiers prowl around those towns all the time. I want to send Mary Beth's description to a friend of mine — a good friend." As he said it, Merritt realized it was true. Summers had always acted the part of a friend, but Merritt had never been able to see that before. "He's a commissary officer" — he grinned — "with the Yankee Army. He can do some unofficial checking and telegraph me the results."

Bell rubbed his chin, finally nodded reluctant agreement. "Sounds reasonable." He rummaged in a desk drawer and pulled out a printed circular. "This is all we have. If she's got a birthmark or anything, it ain't someplace I've seen. One thing, though," he added, still holding the paper, "that telegram comes to me, not to you. Can I trust you for that?"

Merritt hesitated, then said, "All right, Marshal. I'm not trying to tell you how to run your business."

"Why not? Everybody else in town does. Joe Hicks — he's the telegraph operator — hangs out over to Ma Sullivan's. You talk to him, hear?"

"Yes, sir, Marshal. I'll take care of it."

Merritt took the circular and got out before Bell could reconsider. He paused outside to read through it. Mary Beth Rankin, eighteen, tall and blond, sounded like Clint's type, all right. She wasn't Laurie, though, and Clint should have been smart enough to see the differences. Merritt sealed the circular in his letter to Major Summers and dropped it off at the store to be mailed. As he made his way down to Ma Sullivan's stage stand, his certainty grew that he would never find Clint Davidson alive.

The telegraph office was a bare cubicle at one corner of the big log building. Its presence there was almost accidental. The lines followed the stage road, giving fair service to towns along the way when weather or Comanches didn't interrupt, but business in Gilead was bound to be slow.

Merritt pushed through the door and paused to look around. A rough wooden counter divided the room in two. Against the far wall was a table holding an old army telegraph key with its coils and wires. The big glass batteries, their sides stained with spilled acid, crouched under the table.

Nobody seemed to be around, so Merritt found a sheet of paper and a stub of pencil and scribbled a quick message to Summers: DEAR GEORGE — NEED THAT FAVOR NOW — LETTER FOLLOWS — MORE WHEN I SEE YOU — MERRITT. Then he rapped sharply on the counter top with his knuckles.

"Hey. Anybody here?"

"I hear you. Just a minute."

Considerably more than a minute passed, and then the operator came from someplace in the back of the building. He was an old man, with rimless glasses and a puffy-cheeked, peering face that reminded Merritt of some kind of rodent. He pushed the glasses back onto his forehead and squinted at his customer.

"Joe Hicks. What's your business?"

Merritt gave him the blank, adding the major's name and address. He paid for the

222

message, then held up a dollar for Hicks to see.

"There'll be an answer to this – maybe in a week, maybe longer. When it comes in, I want it to go to Marshal Bell, day or night. If he's not in, have it sent to me."

"No extra charge for that," Hicks said.

Merritt pushed the coin across to him. "I know. This is just to help you remember."

"Fair enough." Hicks tucked the dollar into a vest pocket and smiled, the smile making him look more than ever like a gopher. "Don't worry, mister. I'll remember."

For the next few days, Merritt had to keep reminding himself he couldn't expect an answer from Summers right away. Laurie, indeed, didn't think they would hear from him at all.

"Even if you're right about that girl, you don't have any idea where she might be. What are the chances of someone finding her?"

"Well, it's a big army," Merritt said. "George was always the type who had a lot of connections, and this new assignment hasn't changed that. I think our chances are pretty good." He shrugged. "Anyway, she's the only card we have. We may as well play it out."

Laurie set her jaw stubbornly. "I still don't think Clint ran off with her. More likely, he's dead somewhere."

"If he's dead, somebody killed them. Who?"

"How should—" she began angrily, but then she let her voice trail away. She wrinkled her forehead in thought, finally shook her head. "It's no good. I've thought about it before, a lot of nights before you came. Nobody had a reason to kill Clint."

Remembering his meeting with Frank at the Rankin place, Merritt felt a moment's doubt. He didn't say anything, though, and then Troop called from outside.

"Hey, Yank — it's 'most sunup. Time we was getting to work!"

Gradually, Merritt slipped back into the routine of ranch work. He had one message from Summers — "LOOKING" — and then nothing while weeks mounted into a month and more. He and Troop were slowly building the herd to a reasonable size — another fifty head from Tom Drake, a hundred from other ranches, almost as many again picked up unbranded and wild from the Comanche plains to the west. There was work enough to make him forget the search, but now he had a reason to remember.

He was thinking about it one day as he cleaned out a water hole near the boundary of Tom Drake's ranch. A shelf of gray limestone outcropped there at the foot of a bluff, and an ice-cold seep of water crept down its face to form a clear shallow pool. Merritt had worked off and on for three days, enlarging the pool and clearing the heavy brush that choked its bank. Now he was building a rock spillway to keep the overflow from washing out his packed-earth dam.

When he stopped to rest, tired and muddy and shivering from the chill water that soaked his jeans, his mind went back to the Rankin girl. He still hadn't had any report on her. Even if he'd guessed right, the odds against finding her got longer every day. Maybe it was time to give it up. He could leave the ranch for a while — Billy was well able to handle things now — maybe visit San Antonio and find out about the man who'd sold Clint's horse. That trail was long cold, but it would be better than just waiting.

He shook off the thought and went back to work, stooping to pick up another rock for the spillway. The dun, unsaddled and picketed a few yards away, suddenly threw up its head and whickered sharply. Merritt paused, still holding the rock. Listening hard, he heard the ring of shod hooves on the rocky bluff, the scuff and slide of gravel as a horse came down the bank. Setting the stone down gently, he moved back to the place he'd left his carbine.

"Hello!"

Merritt recognized Tom Drake's voice and straightened sheepishly. A moment later, the rancher came into sight around the face of the bluff. His eyes went from Merritt to the rifle and back before he spoke.

"Howdy. Mind if I stop for a drink?"

"Help yourself," Merritt said. He leaned the Spencer back against the rock shelf. "Sorry. I didn't know who you were, at first."

Drake nodded gravely. "Man's got to be careful, out like this," he agreed.

He dismounted and drank, then scooped up a hatful of water for his horse. Tying the reins to a nearby mesquite, he hunkered down in the lush grass along the edge of the pool.

"Looks like you've been busy here," he said. He ran his hands over the unfinished spillway and nodded to himself. "That'll make a right nice little tank."

Merritt squatted beside him. "I thought I'd better fix it up," he said. "We're figuring on moving another fifty head down here from the south valley. I think the grass will support them year-round."

"It should. My cows like it well enough. I was out here looking for strays when I saw your horse." He wiped his palms on his thighs and smiled at Merritt. "You're really getting the place in shape."

"Thanks," Merritt said. "Listen, I've been thinking — next spring, instead of selling our beef to one of the big outfits, we could organize our own drive. Your place and mine, the Allgoods, anybody else who wanted to come in."

Drake ran a hand through his gray hair. "I don't know. That's risky."

"But Kansas prices are five times what we'd get here. I won't be ready to go it alone by then, but among us, we could get up a fairsized herd."

"There's truth in that. I'll think about it." The rancher changed the subject suddenly. "Still having trouble hiring hands?"

Merritt shrugged. "Billy and I manage all right. The others will come around when they see I'm here to stay."

"A young feller was by looking for work the other day. I told him about you. I expect he'll stop in."

"If he's hard up enough to work for a Yank." Merritt's voice was matter-of-fact. The bitterness was all gone now.

"I don't think he'll mind," Drake said, smiling at the tone. "It's about time we all buried the past and got on about our business."

The words brought Merritt back to his thoughts about Clint and the Rankin girl. He could plan for the future, but there could never be a future for him and Laurie until those questions were answered. He scooped up a handful of mud and let it run out between his fingers, watching as the clean water from the spring swept it away.

"I'd like to do that," he said. "But I've got one more job to do. There are some things in the past that won't stay buried."

When he looked up, Drake's smile was gone. The rancher's leathery face seemed drawn and old. There was pain in his blue eyes as he rose to untie his horse.

"I expect you're right, Mr. Merritt," he said softly. "Best I was getting along, now. Jim Bob'll wonder where I am."

It was well past sundown when Merritt rode up the hill overlooking the ranch house. He'd stayed on to finish the stock tank, then swung by Phantom Hill on his way back. He wasn't quite sure why he'd gone there. Something in Drake's words had stirred a vague uneasiness in him, but the ruins of the old fort had given him no clue to their meaning. Something about the War, probably. Merritt was coming to understand that these people had been as badly marked by it as he and Billy.

As he came in sight of the house, Billy Troop was just starting up the hill. The big man saw him and reined up instead, waiting for him by the trail.

"Evening, Yank. Laurie figured for sure the Comanches had got you, so I was coming out to look for the body."

Merritt laughed. "Sorry. I'm still using it." He looked closely at Troop. The big man had a gun belt buckled around his waist, and Laurie's long Walker Colt hung at his side. "I thought you didn't like guns."

Troop touched the big revolver's butt, tugged self-consciously to straighten the belt.

"They come in handy, sometimes. You get held up?"

"Tom Drake stopped by and visited for a while. And I rode past the fort on my way back."

Troop looked quickly at him, but didn't ask any questions. Instead, he said, "Well, while you was out lallygagging, I got the last of those new steers moved over to the valley. Then I chopped about a cord of wood and weeded the garden, and finally decided you weren't never coming home to supper."

"Sorry, Billy." Merritt urged the dun along. "You shouldn't have waited."

"Had to. Laurie wouldn't feed us until you showed up. Oh," he added as an afterthought, "some kid from town brought a telegram by about two hours ago. I gave him — hey, wait up, Yank. What's the matter?"

But Merritt had already put the spurs to the dun and was galloping headlong down the trail toward the house.

CHAPTER 15

Built on a hilltop above the steep-banked Brazos, Fort Griffin was a jumble of temporary huts and white mushroom-shaped Sibley tents. Trenches and piles of cut timber marked spots where permanent buildings were to be. The shouts of officers and the steady din of hammers and saws carried faintly across the river to Merritt's ears.

"We'll have three troops of cavalry in here early next month," George Summers said. "It doesn't look like much now, but just wait."

They'd needed a fort here in the old days, but there was never enough money. Now settlers were pushing farther and farther up the Brazos, into the heart of the Comanche plains. Already a town had sprung up north of Griffin, the kind of town that always followed the Army. That was the place Merritt had come to see.

"What about the girl?" he asked.

"Over there." Leaning across his saddle horn,

Summers pointed. "That big place is Keegan's — he calls it a saloon. She works there. She has a cabin out back, just at the edge of the woods."

"You're certain she's the right one?"

Major Summers looked curiously at him. "Not certain, no," he answered. "She fits the description, and we know she's a runaway."

He waited for Merritt to say something, then added, "We were careful about checking up on her before you got here. If she'd decided to run, I didn't have any grounds to hold her."

Merritt pulled his attention away from the town and turned to Summers.

"Thanks, George," he said quietly. "I know you've had to bend some rules to do this. I appreciate it."

"Think nothing of it." Summers spread his hands casually, though his pleasure showed in his round face. "Just remind me to be careful about offering you favors. Finding one saloon girl out of all the hog ranches on the military frontier was a pretty tall order. Your letter made it sound important, though."

"It is." Merritt had given Summers a brief account of Clint's disappearance. Now he added a few details, finishing with, "I think the girl knows something, something that scared her out of Gilead. Anyway, I want to talk to her."

232

Summers grunted. "Well, talking to her is no problem. The easiest place to meet her will be the saloon, but you'd better get her out of there to ask questions. If she yells for help, you'll have trouble." Summers smiled thinly. "There'll be a couple of troopers in there if you need them — but I don't want a riot."

"I'll be careful," Merritt said. He looked at Summers. "Thanks, George," he repeated. "This means a lot to me — more than just business."

"Ah, hell, forget it." Summers shrugged. "Listen, there's no point in going down there before dark. Ride on over to my quarters, and we'll have a drink first."

Rain began falling just at dusk, a slow, sullen drizzle that turned the raw earth of shantytown into sticky mud. The sun died unseen in the west, and night came, full and dark, before Merritt rode down to dismount in front of Keegan's saloon.

He tied the dun in the meager shelter of the building. Half a dozen other horses stood nearby, snuffling and stamping their feet in weary protest. Yellow light shone dimly through the greased paper of the building's windows. From inside, Merritt heard laughter and the low sounds of conversation. Loosening his Colt in its holster, he crossed the few yards to the door and stepped through.

The place was fairly quiet — a typical night between army paydays, Merritt guessed. It boasted a plank bar and a few rough tables with hand-split stools around them. Not far from the doorway, two buffalo hunters were having some sort of contest that required a great deal of struggling and profanity. Three or four others looked on, placing bets and calling encouragement. A pair of soldiers sat at a table joking with a buxom Mexican girl, and a third trooper, his back wedged into a corner, sipped morosely at a beer. He looked hard at Merritt, then turned his eyes casually toward a blond girl who sat alone at a table toward the back.

Merritt nodded fractionally as he strode over to lean on the bar. He ordered a beer and exchanged a few words with the heavy-browed bartender while he drank half of it. Finally, he motioned toward the blond girl.

"Is the lady busy?"

The barkeep laughed. "Not now, cowboy. Help yourself."

Merritt shoved a coin across the bar. "How about a bottle, then? Something that won't poison us."

"The girls drink house stock," the barkeep said quickly. Merritt drew back the dollar and replaced it with a five-dollar gold piece.

"This ought to cover it," he said. "I hit it big in a poker game, and tonight's my night to howl a little."

The barkeep hesitated, then handed across a bottle. The coin disappeared into his apron. "All right," he said. He lowered his voice. "You'd be smart to take her out of here before those hiders are through funning. They might have some ideas, too."

"Thanks."

Merritt took the bottle and two glasses across to the girl's table. She looked up at him and smiled expectantly, a sly half grin that suggested she was secretly laughing at him or at herself. She had wide blue eyes and a scattering of freckles across her nose. Merritt was surprised to see she wore none of the heavy makeup that most saloon girls favored. Her fair skin and short-cropped golden hair gave her a look — not of innocence; there was too much bitter knowledge in her eyes for that — but of animal freedom, like a young colt just finding its legs. She was Clint's type, all right, Merritt admitted. Out of here, she would be a woman any man might look at twice.

"Hello, cowboy," she said. She crossed her arms and hugged them to her body, watching his face. "Buy me a drink?"

235

"Sure, Mary Beth." Merritt drew back a stool and sat beside her, putting bottle and glasses on the table. "I thought I would. Kind of slow tonight, isn't it?"

"Just like usual. They don't—" Her gaze had followed the bottle, and she'd answered almost automatically. Then suddenly her eyes were narrow and searching, her voice hard. "Hey, how do you know my name? I don't know you!"

Merritt grinned. "I knew you'd forget," he said. "Fickle." He reached across to open the bottle, poured a drink for each of them. "I'm Steve, remember? Back when you worked at the Sultan, over by Fort Mason?"

That was a piece of information Summers had given him, and Merritt hoped it was accurate. Evidently, it came close enough, because Mary Beth's clenched hands opened a little.

"Oh. Oh, yeah, I remember," she said doubtfully. Reaching for the glass, she sipped at it, made a face, drank more deeply. "Anyway, don't call me that here. It's too close — I don't want you to."

"That's fine with me. What should I call you?"

"Whatever you like. But pour me another glass of that."

A fresh burst of talk and laughter from the buffalo hunters made them both look up. One of the men reeled across to the bar, then returned, his arms loaded with bottles.

"Maybe we ought to go someplace else while they're busy," Merritt suggested. "I've got a little money, and I figured I could spend it on you."

Mary Beth giggled, looking at the group of hunters. "I thought we'd wait. They like me, too." She looked at him teasingly, leaning back so that the thin shirtwaist she wore pulled tight across the curves of her body. "Would you fight for me, Steve?"

"I'd lose." Merritt made to rise. "Still, if you'd rather pass the time with one of them than me—"

"Got a good opinion of yourself, don't you, cowboy?" She caught his hand and pulled herself up, capturing the bottle. "All right. My place is right out back." She snuggled against him and smiled. "Maybe I'll remember you better there."

Merritt steered her to the door and out into the darkness. The rain had stopped. The clouds were breaking up now, allowing fitful moonlight to seep through. Merritt paused for a breath of night air free of smoke and whiskey fumes, but Mary Beth tugged at his arm.

"Over this way," she said. "C'mon, cowboy." The drinks had hit her quickly. She clung heavily to him, picking her way uncertainly across the muddy ground. Merritt let her lead him around the side of the saloon toward her cabin. He'd have to be careful, he thought. There was no knowing how she might react when she found out who he really was. Maybe the best way—

"Don't be so quiet." Mary Beth shook his shoulder. She giggled. "You thinking about what we're going to do?"

"That's right."

She laughed and stretched to kiss his cheek. He pulled away a little, almost without realizing it.

"Don't be shy."

They had come out of the shadow of the saloon into the open moonlit space behind it. Mary Beth stopped suddenly and reached up to grab Merritt around the neck. As she turned, her foot slipped in the wet grass and she fell, pulling him to one knee.

"Oh! You could at least wait—"

Her words were lost in the crash of a rifle. The muzzle blast tore the night apart, and Merritt heard the snapping passage of the bullet close by his head. He reacted with sheer instinct. Straightening his left arm, he sent Mary Beth sprawling to the ground while he pivoted on his knee, his right hand dipping smoothly to the cut-down holster. The shot had come from the shadows maybe thirty yards away. Merritt put three bullets into the spot, left, right, and center, before he fully realized the gun was in his hand. On his third shot, the rifle roared again, this time into the air.

Merritt fired once more, a couple of feet below the flash. Then he was running, heading off on a slant toward the source of the shots. He didn't see anyone, but his foot touched something heavy and still. Reaching down, he put his hand full on the bearded face of a man.

For a moment, he stayed there motionless. He heard Mary Beth's screams behind him, turned to see her on hands and knees in the mud. Then a crowd pushed out of the saloon, one of the soldiers in the lead with a lantern.

"Over here," Merritt called. Drawing a deep breath, he holstered the pistol. That holster rig worked pretty well, he thought absently. He'd have to tell the marshal.

The soldier brought the lantern over, most of the crowd from the saloon clustered behind him. Mary Beth cut off her screams and ran across to Merritt. Together, they looked down at the body on the ground. The man had been hit twice and was quite dead. The face, turned open-eyed to the night sky, belonged to Baldy Witherspoon.

"He tried to bushwhack us," Merritt said. He looked on the ground, found the heavy buffalo gun. "He should've used a pistol."

After one look at the dead man, Mary Beth had squeezed her eyes shut and hidden her face against Merritt's shoulder. He felt her trembling and put an arm around her.

"Anybody know him?" the bartender asked, pushing forward. He looked around the silent circle, then returned to Merritt. "Well, you killed him, you better bury him. He's too ugly to leave lying here."

"I'll take care of it."

Major Summers had come up on the crowd without being seen. His voice was quiet and authoritative, and he was flanked by a pair of armed troopers. He gestured at Merritt and the girl.

"You two, come along."

"Hey, you can't arrest him." That was one of the buffalo hunters. "He's a citizen. This ain't the Army's business."

"Now it is. Move along."

The other soldiers in the group had drawn apart. The hiders weighed the odds, then began to drift back toward the saloon, still grumbling. The barkeep and the soldiers followed. Summers let out a long sigh.

"You always did make life interesting, Steve,"

he said. "Good to see you haven't changed. Do you know this fellow?"

"He hangs around Gilead. I've had trouble with him before."

"I see," the major said. "Funny thing is, I know him, too." He knelt over Witherspoon's body and pulled back the dead man's sleeve. A long scar puckered the forearm. "That's him, all right. You remember me telling you about that bunch of Rebs we chased from Kansas, right at the end of the War?"

"I remember."

"We captured their rear guard. Four men." Summers looked up at Merritt, his face grim. "He was one of them. Quite a coincidence, wouldn't you say?"

It was past midnight when Merritt left the major's tent. Even with the absence of law in the shantytown, Summers hadn't been comfortable about the shooting. He'd asked a lot of questions, but Merritt didn't have many answers. Finally, he'd agreed to take it up again the next morning, after Merritt had talked to the girl.

Mary Beth was in the adjutant's shack, under the guard of one of the soldiers Merritt had seen earlier. Her skirt and shirtwaist were torn and streaked with mud, and she looked very young and bedraggled. She ran to Merritt and threw her arms around him when he came to claim her. All the way back through the quiet town, she gripped his arm tightly. Not until they were inside her cabin, with the door closed and the lamp lighted, did she draw away.

"Oh, Steve." She sniffed and wiped her nose with the back of her hand, little-girl fashion. "Wait. I need a handkerchief."

The room was sparsely furnished, holding only a washstand, a sagging bed, and a big upright chest. Mary Beth went to the chest and reached into the top drawer. When she turned, she held a vicious little rimfire pistol. All trace of childishness and fear was gone from her face.

"You're not any cowboy," she said coldly. "You're friends with that Yankee major. What do you want with me?"

Merritt looked at her, then smiled wryly. He should have guessed — she hadn't really struck him as the kind who would come to pieces.

"I'm a friend of Clint Davidson's," he said. There was no point in lying now. "I want you to tell me where he is."

Her eyes widened slightly, but that was all.

"I don't know any Clint Davidson." She raised the gun. "Don't think you can take me back to Gilead. I could shoot you right now, and nobody would care."

"My friend the major might." Merritt let her think about that for a second, then added, "I don't plan to take you back. But Clint's family would like to know what's happened to him."

The girl's eyes blazed. "His family. His wife, you mean! Why should I worry about her?"

"Do you worry about yourself? Somebody just tried to kill you," Merritt said softly. He wasn't sure which of them Baldy had been shooting at, but Mary Beth seemed to believe him. "If I'd gotten here an hour later, you'd be dead. The next time, I might not be around."

"The next time, they won't find me."

"I found you, and so did Baldy. You're dangerous to somebody. They aren't likely to forget it. If you'll tell me the truth, maybe I can help."

"Sure!" She laughed bitterly. "You just want to help me! What do you get out of it?"

"I find out about Clint. You were with him the night he disappeared, weren't you?"

"It wasn't my fault," she said quickly. For an instant, her face was young and vulnerable again, but then the mask came back. She studied him, her forehead creased in a frown. "Maybe you're right," she murmured. "What have I got to lose?"

She tossed the gun carelessly back into the drawer — Merritt winced, but it didn't go off — then went to sit on the edge of the bed.

"Come on," she said, patting the space beside her. "Sit here, where I can see you. Ask your questions."

"Just one question. What happened that night?"

"It started before that," she said. "Clint and me, we were — you know — together some before he brought that wife of his out. After that, he — I broke it off." She tossed her head. "I wouldn't have any truck with a married man."

Merritt couldn't help himself. "Wasn't he just as married before Laurie came out?" he asked.

"You wouldn't have thought so." Mary Beth laughed, a soft, feline sound. "Anyhow, things at home got bad, and I decided to light out. I had to. Pa was—" She stopped, then shrugged and continued. "I figured Clint would help me. I got him word what I was doing, and he said he'd meet me that night out at the old fort. We'd spent some time there."

She was silent a long time, her fingers picking at the coverlet. When she resumed, her voice was softer.

"It was raining. I'd got what money I could and Pa's old horse. Clint was waiting for me. We talked a minute — just talked — and then we heard some noises. There was a light, too —

a lantern, I guess. Clint said something about rustlers and told me to stay where I was, and he spurred that big horse of his over that way. Then there was yelling and people were shooting, and — and that's all I saw."

"What did you do?"

"I lit out." She looked at him defiantly. "Wouldn't've done no good for me to get shot, too. What else could I do?"

Merritt didn't answer her. "Did you recognize any of the men?" he asked.

The girl shook her head, tight-lipped. "Didn't even see how many there were. Three or four, I suppose." She leaned back on her elbows and stretched, looking sideways at him. "Now that's all I know. Satisfied?"

"Yeah." Merritt rose. Reaching into his pocket, he counted out five double eagles. The heavy coins clinked solidly together as he dropped them on the bed. "Catch the stage tomorrow, Mary Beth. Get out of Texas. You'll be safe enough."

Her hand closed like a claw on the money. "I'll do that," she said, her eyes shining. "I always wanted to see Kansas City."

Merritt started for the door, but her soft voice stopped him.

"Steve?" She licked her lips and smiled at him the way she'd smiled in the saloon. "You can stay if you want to, Steve. It might be nice."

Slowly, Merritt shook his head. "No, thanks. I have to get back to the major."

The girl sniffed. "Your loss," she said. "So long, cowboy."

"Good luck, Mary Beth."

But Merritt had the feeling that wherever Mary Beth Rankin went, her luck would never be very good.

"I still can't understand why you let the girl go!" Major Summers paused in his pacing to shake his head at Merritt. "She's the key to the whole thing! Without her, you have no evidence at all."

Merritt rubbed his eyes and fought back a yawn. He'd had a long night, and the morning wasn't starting out much better. He'd intentionally waited until the stage pulled out to repeat Mary Beth's story to the major, and Summers hadn't appreciated that a bit.

"She'd helped all she could, George," he said gently. "Clint's dead — I'm sure of it now. I wanted her out of this before somebody killed her, too."

"But suppose there's trouble over that shooting last night? Her testimony—"

"You know what her testimony would be worth in court," Merritt interrupted. "Besides, this is a military reservation and you're the ranking officer. I used to know a George Summers who didn't worry so much about legalities."

Summers tried to hold his stern expression. "Now, listen—" Then, surprisingly, he broke off and laughed. "That George Summers was a stupid young captain who liked to fight," he said ruefully. "Not a fat commissary major holding out for retirement. Maybe I've changed more than I'd thought."

"Not so much," Merritt said. "If you see that young captain, ask him why he chased a bunch of Johnny Rebs all the way from Kansas to Phantom Hill. That was a long way to ride just because they'd raided a supply depot."

Summers sank down on a stool at his field desk and pondered for a minute. "I've thought about that," he said. "We had orders to get them, no matter what. I never knew why. But I can try to find out, if you think it's important."

"I think it might be. That hardcase last night was one of your Rebs, and he wanted me dead for some reason. Maybe he was tied in with Clint, too."

"I thought it was the girl he wanted." Summers raised his eyebrows. "You think he was after you?"

Merritt spread his hands. "Who knows?" he

said. "But I have a better question. How did he know either of us was here? As soon as you're through dressing me down, I figure to go back to Gilead and find out."

The major chuckled. "All right, Mr. Merritt. You're free to go." His face turned grave as Merritt rose to leave. "Watch yourself, Steve. Somebody is serious about this."

Merritt nodded grimly. "They'd better be," he said. "I am."

CHAPTER 16

It was late afternoon, and the main street of Gilead was quiet. Almost alone on the boardwalk, Merritt strode casually past shuttered businesses and the two noisy saloons toward Ma Sullivan's stage stand. The stage stand would be busy now, he knew, serving meals in the long whitewashed dining room. He glanced quickly around, but nobody seemed to be paying him much attention. That was fine. He'd purposely come in late enough so that he wouldn't attract much notice.

"Hey, Yank!"

The hoarse whisper caught him as he started across the alley beside Ma Sullivan's place. He turned sharply into it. Billy Troop was waiting in the shadows.

"I been waiting on you, Yank. You're running late."

Merritt nodded, glancing around the darkened alley. "I left the wagon over at the store to be loaded with supplies," he said. "Frank came out of the marshal's office as I was driving into town. He seemed sort of surprised to see me, but he didn't make any trouble. Are you sure Marshal Bell's still over at Willow Springs?"

"I told you he was," Troop said patiently. "He's delivering a prisoner over there, and him and Sheriff Beasley will likely yarn most of the night. He won't be back 'til sometime tomorrow." The big man shifted his weight uneasily. "I still think you should've talked to him about this."

"Maybe."

They'd argued that out before, with Merritt insisting they wait until Bell was away. The marshal might well be the one who'd sent Baldy to kill him. Until he knew a few more answers, Merritt couldn't afford to trust anyone too far.

He had few enough answers now. He'd tried to think the whole thing through on his long ride back from Fort Griffin. Clint had stumbled on something important enough to get him killed, important enough so that men were still willing to kill for it. Baldy had been involved somehow, and there had to be a trail leading from him to those shadowy others Mary Beth had seen. That was the trail Merritt meant to follow.

Troop inclined his head toward the stage

stand. "You just about made it in time. Joe closed the telegraph office a little while ago. Usually, he takes his supper here, then walks home."

Merritt looked back along the alley. "What's back there?"

"Well, there's the stables. That's all."

"That's enough. I'd like about five minutes in there with Mr. Hicks."

"Sure," Troop said. Then he looked closely at Merritt. "You ain't going to hurt him, are you? He's a good enough old man."

"I'm not going to hurt him. I just want to ask him who saw that telegram about the Rankin girl. That's the only way Baldy could have found out where she was."

"I guess."

Troop still didn't sound convinced. What was it Marshal Bell had said long ago about Billy? "He came back from the War without much sense, but he's good at judging people as an old hound dog." If Billy trusted Bell, the chances were Bell deserved it.

"It'll be all right, Billy," Merritt said. "We'll tell the marshal as soon as he gets back. And right after we talk to Mr. Hicks, we can head on home."

"Yeah," Troop said. "Home." He looked up suddenly at Merritt and grinned. "Has a right

251

good sound to it, don't it, Yank?"

Merritt nodded sober agreement. The ranch was home, now — his home. He hadn't really been conscious of that until two days ago, when he'd come back from Fort Griffin.

He'd circled wide around Gilead, not wanting to be seen, and had come up the long valley to the east of Phantom Hill. Lost in his thoughts, he'd hardly noticed the dun starting up the rise that overlooked the ranch house. On the crest, though, he reined in and sat motionless with the buildings spread below him.

It was early evening. The sky still showed gold and orange from the sunset, and a single bright star hung in the west, far out over the plains. Shadows already lay deep around the bunkhouse and barn. From the windows of the house, light spilled yellow and warm and welcoming into the gathering dark. For the first time, Merritt knew what it meant to have a place like that to come back to, to have people — to have Laurie — waiting for him.

Then the dun tossed its head and neighed, fighting the reins. His mood broken, Merritt laughed.

"You've got the right idea, big boy. Let's get down there and get to the barn."

As he rode into the yard, Laurie came out

on the porch, peering into the dark.

"Billy? Is that — Steve! You're back!"

He dismounted and took two steps to meet her, sweeping her slender body into an embrace. They held each other for a long time without speaking.

"I thought it was Billy," she said finally. "He and Jory are out working on the south range." When Merritt didn't answer, she pulled back from him, looking up into his face. "You found her, didn't you?" she asked quietly. "And now you know about Clint."

It wasn't really a question. Merritt inclined his head.

"He's dead. I'm sure, now. Before long, we'll find the ones that did it."

Laurie let out a long breath and covered her face with her hands. Merritt put his arms around her to comfort her, but when she raised her head, her eyes were dry.

"You'll have to tell me," she said. "All of it. Unsaddle your horse and wash up. Supper's waiting, and I'll fix some coffee. We can talk then." She made to move away, but Merritt tightened his grip and she settled contentedly against him. "I was afraid for you, Steve. I'm glad you're back."

"Me, too," Merritt said. "It's good to be home."

"Yank?" Troop nudged Merritt sharply, bringing him back to the present. "He'll be coming out any minute. You best get back to the barn. I'll bring him along directly."

Merritt made his way back along the alley to the door of the stable. Its iron hinges grated in protest as he eased it open, but nobody was around to hear. Leaving the door open enough to admit a man, he eased inside. The interior was almost completely dark, and the only sounds were the restless pawing and shifting of the horses in the stalls. Satisfied, he slid into the shadows by the doorway and settled down to wait.

The wait wasn't long. Only a couple of minutes had passed when he heard movement outside, and then the scratchy voice of the telegraph operator.

"—don't see what's so important, Billy. What do you want to show me—?"

The words cut off abruptly as Merritt snaked an arm through the doorway and hauled him inside. With a quick warning to Troop to watch the alley, Merritt slammed the door and turned to face Joe Hicks.

"What — what's the meaning — I don't — that is, I don't have much money. I'm—"

"It's not a robbery, Mr. Hicks." Merritt stepped closer to the little man, leaning down to see him better in the dimness. "I just need a word with you in private. I want to ask you about a telegram."

"A telegram?"

Hicks fumbled to straighten his glasses. His hands still trembled a little, Merritt noted, but his tone was more curious than frightened now. He finally got the glasses adjusted on his nose and peered up at Merritt. Abruptly, a look of surprised recognition broke over his face.

"Why, Mr. Merritt! I thought I knew your voice. You gave me a real turn, there." He spread his hands, his gesture taking in Merritt and the darkened barn. "But what did you want to pull me in here for? If you wanted to talk, my office—"

"I sent a telegram not long ago," Merritt interrupted. "You were told to deliver it to me or the marshal, nobody else — but somebody else saw it. I want to know how that happened. Right now."

Hicks stared at him open-mouthed, his plump cheeks working. Then he suddenly straightened, jabbing a finger at Merritt excitedly.

"That telegram! I knew there'd be trouble over that. I told him what you'd said, but he said mind my own business. I told him."

"Easy there. Slow down." In spite of himself, Merritt had to smile at the old man's excitement. "You told who?"

"Why, Frank, of course — you know, Frank Harmon, the marshal's deputy."

"I know, all right. What happened?"

"Well, when your answer came, I took it over to the marshal's, just like you said. He'd gone for the day, but Frank was there and said he'd take it. I didn't want him to, but—" Hicks paused and made a helpless gesture. "Anyway, he read it and said he'd take care of it and for me not to worry, and when I tried to argue, he said mind my own business. Imagine, saying that to me!"

Merritt nodded, inwardly cursing himself for an idiot. He should have known. Frank. Billy had tried to tell him it couldn't be Bell.

"But somebody sent me word anyway," he said. "Did Frank do that?"

"Well, no." The old man looked down at the straw at his feet. "I got to thinking about it, and it just didn't seem right to leave things that way. Finally I decided to send a boy out to your place with a copy." He peered up anxiously at Merritt. "That's all, Mr. Merritt. Did I do right?"

"Just right, Mr. Hicks," Merritt said. "You probably saved a woman's life." He swung the door back, cutting off the man's questions. "Billy! Billy Troop!"

"I'm here, Yank." Troop materialized out of the shadows and ambled over. "Everything all right?"

"Just fine. And it'll be a lot better after I've talked to our friend the deputy." He paused, turned to pump the telegraph operator's hand. "Thank you, Mr. Hicks. You've been a big help. Come on, Billy."

Leaving Hicks with one hand raised in a hesitant farewell, he and Troop strode down the alley and turned toward the marshal's office.

Frank wasn't in town. A few questions revealed he'd ridden south not long after Merritt had seen him. "Seemed to be in an awful hurry," Sid Culver said. "Just saddled his horse and took out at a gallop. Didn't even say good evening."

"Well, that about beats all," Troop said as they walked back toward the store. "What do you think we ought to do, Yank?"

Merritt had been thinking about that. Everything had to fit together somehow — Clint's death and Phantom Hill and the telegram and Major Summers' story about the Rebel raiders. For the first time, Merritt thought he could see part of the pattern.

"Billy, if I wanted to find out about somebody in town, who should I talk to? After the marshal, I mean."

Troop thought for a moment, then laughed. "Aw, that's easy," he said. "Your friend the banker. Old Whitlock, he knows every time somebody sneezes, and he's there to sell them a handkerchief. Reckon that's how he stays so rich."

"I'd better go see him, then. If you want to start back to the ranch, I'll bring the wagon along later."

"Oh, no," Troop said. "I seen this much, and I don't understand a bit of it. Reckon I'll wait and watch the rest."

Banker Whitlock's home stood back away from the main street, surrounded by a high plank fence. The house was dark, but when Merritt swung open the creaking wooden gate, an upstairs window slid open.

"Who's there?"

Remembering the banker's shotgun, Merritt answered quickly. "Steve Merritt. I hate to bother you at night, but it's important. Can we talk to you?"

"Why — of course." There was a pause while Whitlock struck a light. "Just a minute. I'll be right down."

Whitlock was as good as his word. Little more than a minute passed before the front door opened and he stuck his head out, peering around cautiously.

"Come in, Mr. Merritt, Billy."

Inside the hall, Merritt was surprised to see a tall, middle-aged woman on the stairs. She held a lamp in one hand, while the other clutched a long robe together at her throat.

"I don't think you've met my wife," Whitlock said. "Dear, this is Mr. Merritt. You know Billy Troop."

"Good evening, gentlemen." She seemed to accept their presence as a normal part of business — maybe it was, Merritt thought. "I'm sure you'll want to talk to Abel. If you'll just give me a minute, I'll have some coffee ready."

"Thank you, ma'am," Troop said politely. "Me and the Yank would like that fine."

Whitlock frowned, but ushered them through another door.

"I have an office here. Now, what can I do for you?"

"You can give me some information," Merritt said. "Billy says you know the background on almost everybody in town. There's something I have to know about Frank Harmon."

"Well, I don't know." The banker rubbed his chin thoughtfully. From the look he shot at Troop, he didn't much like the whole idea. "I have — ah — certain knowledge of the people I deal with, true. But you wouldn't want me talking about your private affairs. It would be highly improper."

Merritt waved that aside. "It isn't like that," he said. "And I think I know most of it already. The marshal told me once that Frank was with the Home Guard in the War, and that only four of his company came back."

"Why, yes." Whitlock looked bewildered. "I'd heard about that, of course." He made a modest gesture. "These stories get around, but—" He stopped, and his voice hardened. "Why?"

"I'd guess that I know three of those four — Frank, and Baldy Witherspoon, and Adam Garvey. Is that right?"

"Well — yes. Quite a coincidence, all of them being in Gilead. I'd never thought of that. But I still don't see—"

"Who's the fourth one?"

Whitlock hesitated, looking from Merritt to Troop and back. After a moment, he shook his head.

"Well, I don't pretend to understand, but I can't see what it could hurt to tell you. It was another local man — you know him. It was Tom Drake."

CHAPTER 17

The Drake ranch was strangely quiet. No lights showed from the bunkhouse, but Merritt wasn't inclined to take chances. He dismounted and tied Billy's bay well away from the wagon ruts leading up to the corral. He'd taken the horse and sent Troop back to the LJ with the wagon, much against the big man's will.

"It's just plain foolish to go out there by yourself, Yank," Troop had said. "If you're dead set on not waiting for the marshal, you better let me come along. You and me can handle about anything, I reckon."

"That's right, but I don't figure to get in trouble. Nobody's going to be looking for me out at Drake's tonight. What I want you to do is go back and take care of Laurie and Jory. Frank knows that Baldy didn't get me, and there's no telling what he might do next."

"Yank—" Troop's face was twisted into an unhappy frown. He put both hands to his head and pressed his fingers into his temples. "I know you're plumb wrong, but I ain't smart enough to argue with you." Then he looked up suddenly. "You figure they might try to hurt Jory — or Laurie?"

"I don't know," Merritt said. "But I'm sure nobody will hurt them if you're around. I'm counting on you, Billy."

Troop nodded slowly. "You are, ain't you?" he said, half to himself. He straightened and set the big Walker more firmly in its holster. "All right, Yank. You go on and be a hero. I'll see nothing don't happen to them."

Thinking of it now, Merritt had the uncomfortable suspicion Billy might have been right. Coming out here alone didn't seem nearly as smart as it had in town. Still, it would be midday tomorrow before Marshal Bell could be back, and Frank wasn't likely to wait patiently for Merritt to tell the marshal his story. When you knew the enemy was about to act, it was always a good idea to act first. Drake's ranch seemed like the best place to start.

Leaving the bay, Merritt eased forward, keeping to the shadows, the Spencer charged and cocked in his hands. He didn't know what he might find in that silent ranch house, but he meant to be ready.

The bunkhouse still appeared deserted, and the corral beside the barn was empty. A lone horse stood in front of the house, saddled and with its head drooping. Merritt came up cautiously, touched its lathered flank. Someone had ridden in not long before. With a grim face, Merritt moved to circle the house.

The windows were closed and shuttered. Only one gleam of light leaked through, from the room Drake used as an office. Satisfied that no one was outside, Merritt slipped silently across the porch and put his eye to the crack in the shutters.

The thickness of the heavy oak planks restricted his vision, but he could see enough. The room had been wrecked. Its heavy furniture was overturned and papers littered the floor. One man was stretched motionless beside the desk, while another knelt over him, his back toward the window.

With two long strides, Merritt reached the front of the house. The door was ajar. Merritt kicked it open and went in fast, the Spencer held ready at his hip.

"Hold it!"

The kneeling man twisted to face Merritt. The sight of the carbine froze him there. To Merritt's surprise, it was neither Adam Garvey nor Frank. Jim Bob Drake knelt beside his father, his face wet with tears.

"Go ahead, shoot me," he said through

clenched teeth. "After what you've done to my pa, you'd better."

"Jim Bob." Tom Drake's voice was low, his words slurred. "No. Not him." The old man reached out feebly and caught at the boy's shoulder. "Not him."

His anger forgotten, Jim Bob leaned over his father. Merritt put aside the carbine, taking time to close and bolt the door before moving up beside him. Tom Drake's face was cut and bloody, and purple welts showed along his cheek and through the thin gray hair on the side of his head. He'd been beaten terribly — probably pistol-whipped, Merritt thought — but he was conscious. His pain-filled blue eyes looked past the boy into Merritt's.

"Afraid they'd got you." Blood trickled from the corner of his mouth as he spoke. "Two of them. You know?"

"I know." Merritt spoke softly, reaching out gently to ease Drake back to the floor. "You rest for a minute." To Jim Bob, he said, "Get some water, quick. Towels, anything we can use for a bandage. This cut on his temple's pretty deep." When the boy hesitated, Merritt gave him an impatient shove. "Hurry!"

Merritt had tended wounded men before, and with Jim Bob's help, he made a quick job of washing and dressing Drake's injuries. While they were working, the old man's eyes closed and he went off into sleep or unconsciousness. Jim Bob looked fearfully at Merritt.

"Is he — will he be all right?"

"I don't know. None of this will kill him, but we can't tell how much he's hurt inside. No, we'd better not move him. What happened here?"

Jim Bob spread his hands. "I'd been in town for the evening. Nobody was around when I came back — all the hands were gone. Then I heard something inside, so I went in and found him. I'd just been there a minute when you showed up." His voice sharpened, and he grabbed Merritt's arm. "You told him you knew who did this. Who was it?"

Merritt shook him off. "Later," he said. "Right now, you'd better think about taking care of him."

The night was far gone when Tom Drake woke again. He sipped a little water that Jim Bob held to his lips, then looked around him with alert and knowing eyes.

"They haven't come back?" he asked Merritt.

"No. Do you think they will?"

"I guess not. When I wouldn't go along—" He stopped, raised a hand to touch the bruises on his face. "I didn't know they'd sent Baldy to kill you. When Frank got here, Garvey sent

265

my ranch hands away — said it was my orders. He figured something had happened to Baldy."

"Something did." Merritt hesitated, looking at the old man. He didn't want to ask, but he knew it had to be done. "Mr. Drake, what happened to Clint?"

There was a muffled exclamation of surprise from Jim Bob. Drake shifted his gaze to his son, then closed his eyes and shook his head painfully.

"Hadn't wanted it to come out. Guess it's got to, now. How much do you know?"

"A little. Not enough. You'd better go back to the start."

"The start?" Drake's grunt might have been meant for a laugh. "Started in the War, like everything else. We were up to Missouri for Price's campaign in '65. It fell apart, and we rode back for Texas — nigh fifty of us, all there was of the Third Mounted Rifles."

He paused for so long it seemed he'd fallen unconscious again. "You raided a supply depot in Kansas," Merritt prompted gently.

"We did." Drake opened his eyes and tried to raise himself on one elbow. His voice was stronger now. "We needed food and powder. Got it, too, but we never figured on what else we got. And we had Yanks behind us the rest of the way, pushing hard.

"The captain dropped six men off for a rear guard, just up by the Clear Fork. The rest was going on to hide it. One of them knew this country and the old fort, and they meant to bury it there. Garvey – he was a sergeant – he knew where. But the Yanks got us – four of us, anyways – and the Comanches got the rest."

Merritt looked a question at Jim Bob, got a helpless shrug in return.

"Bury what? What were you hiding?"

"Them Yanks at the supply depot was buying cattle from Mexico," Drake said. "They had gold. Thirty thousand dollars in good Yankee gold."

The rest of the story was simple enough. By this time, Merritt knew almost enough to piece it together himself. The four survivors had been sent to a prison camp at Galveston. Months passed while the federal authorities decided whether to treat them as soldiers or bandits. Released at last, they had come back one by one to Gilead – to find Clint and Laurie squatting almost on top of their treasure.

"I wanted to tell Clint right off," Drake said. "He seemed like a fair man. The others wouldn't have it, though – figured we could sneak around without cutting Clint in. Then Clint stumbled on us one night, and Baldy—"

"Hush, Pa!" Jim Bob looked defiantly at Merritt. "Don't you say any more."

Tom Drake shook his head sadly. "It's too late, son. It never rested easy on me, knowing Clint was lying out there." He reached to touch the boy's hand. "I kept it quiet — for you, mostly, I guess. But I won't have another killing. I want you to ride and find the marshal."

"Pa." Jim Bob bowed his head over the old man's hand, and his shoulders shook in a racking sob. "I'm sorry, Pa."

"They thought they could run you out," Drake continued, talking to Merritt. "Tried it a couple of times, right after you came. I kept quiet about that, too. Finally convinced them you'd settle in and they could work around you. Then you set out to find Clint." He closed his eyes. "That's all."

"Where are they now?" Merritt asked softly.

"Out laying for you." Drake gave his grunting laugh again. "Be a good joke on them if they knowed you were here. Frank said you had the wagon in town, and they were going to bushwhack you on the way home, out by Phantom Hill."

He chuckled, but Merritt's face had gone dead-white. "Oh, my God!" He jumped to his feet, grabbing for the Spencer.

"What is it, Yank?" Jim Bob asked, staring at him wide-eyed. "You look like—"

"Get the marshal. I'm going to Phantom Hill. Billy Troop left town about the time I did, driving the wagon. He must have gotten there hours ago."

Light grew in the eastern sky behind Merritt as he spurred the bay at a killing pace toward Phantom Hill. The sun rose, throwing a long shadow of man and horse out ahead of him, while the night animals sought their burrows and the first birds began to sing. Merritt rode in desperate silence, the Spencer across his saddlebow, his body leaning into the bay as if this was a cavalry charge. From the first, he knew he'd be too late.

He saw the wagon as he reached the outlying buildings of the old fort. It had gone off the road and overturned just short of the roofless shell of the guardhouse. The team must have pulled free of the broken shafts and run for home, because they were nowhere to be seen. Nothing moved among the ruins.

Merritt reined his mount in sharply and flung out of the saddle. Crouching low, the carbine ready, he worked past the gaunt chimneys until he reached the spot.

A few yards from the wagon, a heavy growth

of some low, spreading plant covered the ground. The plant had grayish-green leaves and tiny yellow flowers. The dull red of dried blood lay like paint across the gray and yellow. Merritt followed the blood and the trail of crushed and broken foliage. Billy Troop had dragged himself a dozen yards from the road and into a little fold in the ground. Merritt found him there, facedown and motionless, his right hand still locked around the walnut butt of the Walker Colt.

The sharp scent of crushed leaves stung Merritt's eyes as he knelt beside the big man. He gripped Troop's wrist, completely without hope, then caught his breath in surprise. There was a pulse, weak and thready, as though it didn't have much blood to work with. Troop was alive.

Gently, Merritt grasped the wide shoulders, turned him over. He'd expected Troop to be unconscious, but his blue eyes flickered open. Troop's forehead wrinkled in momentary puzzlement, and then a weak grin pulled at his mouth.

"Hey, Yank," he whispered. "I figured you'd come. Been waiting for you."

"Don't talk."

Merritt tore away the blood-soaked shirt. Troop had been shot twice, low in the chest.

The wounds weren't bleeding much now, but they were bad.

"Gotta talk," Troop objected. "There was two of them, Yank. Hid out over by the guardhouse. Loosed off at me before I saw them." He grimaced and lifted the Walker a trifle. "Kind of hoped they'd come to finish the job, but they rode out. Went toward town."

Merritt had been busy while the big man spoke, ripping strips from his own shirt and folding them into bandages. Now he straightened.

"I'm going to bring up my horse, Billy. I'll get you into town."

Troop laughed, a low throaty chuckle that ended in a bout of soundless coughing.

"Hell, Yank," he said. "I ain't going nowhere. You know that. You've surely seen enough fellers shot that you know when one's going to die."

"Billy," Merritt said helplessly. He knew with sick certainty that Troop was right. It was just like the War — any time he got close to someone, death was there too. "Billy, it's me they were after. This is all my fault."

"Ain't nothing your fault but taking me out of that saloon," Troop said. "Always meant to thank you for that." Merritt started to speak, but Troop caught his wrist in a surprisingly tight grip. "It ain't like the War, Yank," he said. "We been thinking that too long. I got in this because I wanted to — just like you."

The coughing hit him again. When it cleared, he said, "Yank, after you get the ones who shot me—"

"Sure, Billy."

"—take Jory fishing some. He—"

He caught a sudden sharp breath, let it out slowly. Merritt leaned closer.

"What, Billy?"

Troop didn't answer. The harsh lines of his face were relaxed into a childlike smile. After a moment, Merritt reached down gently and closed the wide blue eyes.

Merritt stayed there a long time, head bowed, hardly conscious of his nails digging into his palms or of the ragged breaths that tore through his chest. Rising to his feet at last, he yanked a heavy tarp from beneath the overturned wagon. He spread it over Troop's body and anchored it firmly with rocks. That was the best he could do for the moment. The bay was skittish from the blood and the smell of death, but Merritt quieted him and mounted.

As he turned toward Gilead, his mouth was clamped into a thin, bloodless line. Troop had said this wasn't like the War. Well, he was right. Frank Harmon and Adam Garvey weren't part of any army, and they weren't fighting for a cause. They'd killed for profit — senselessly, because Clint would have dealt fairly with them if he'd known the truth — and now they'd killed a second time, out of fear.

Another thing was different, too. The murderers had names and faces, and Merritt figured he knew where to find them. They hadn't come close enough last night to know they'd shot the wrong man. They'd be in town, acting innocent, expecting to get away with this as they'd gotten away with shooting Clint.

That was the last difference. This time, they were going to answer for it — to him.

CHAPTER 18

Merritt brought the bay into Gilead at a walk, holding exactly to the middle of the road, the Spencer ready in his right hand. He reined in at the head of the main street and studied its length, then went on to the livery stable. Sid Culver was just swinging back the wide doors for the morning.

"Howdy, Yank," he said affably. "You're up early. How's that bay working out for you?"

Dismounting, Merritt threw him the reins.

"Has Marshal Bell come back yet?"

"Ain't seen him," Culver said. "He'd come by here to leave his horse, so I reckon he's still off visiting. You looking to talk to him?"

"I'm looking for Adam Garvey and Frank Harmon. Are they in town?"

Culver raised his head at the tone of the question, studied Merritt for a long minute. Merritt rubbed the back of one hand across his mouth. He knew how he must look, dirty and travel-stained, with drawn face and red-rimmed eyes. He was tired, and his voice sounded strange in his own ears. Even so, he returned the blacksmith's gaze steadily and coldly, and he still held the carbine. Whatever Culver may have thought, he dropped his eyes and answered.

"I saw Garvey a while ago — early for him, too. He was down to Ma Sullivan's for breakfast. Frank's most likely at the marshal's office."

"Thanks."

Culver started to lead the bay back into the interior of the stable. Then he stopped, looking back at Merritt.

"Say, Yank," he said carefully, "if you want to see the marshal, maybe you better wait for him right here. You could lie down in one of the stalls in back. You don't look too good."

Merritt laughed harshly. Until that moment, he'd intended to wait for the marshal, but now he saw that was a mistake. He didn't know when Bell might get back — didn't know for sure that Jim Bob would bring him, in fact. Meanwhile, Frank and Garvey were running loose.

He'd figured they would lie low, thinking him dead. That was no sure thing, though. And sooner or later, someone would stumble across Troop's body out by Phantom Hill and come rushing into town with the news. Then the killers would know they'd gotten the wrong man.

Slowly, Merritt shook his head. Garvey and Frank — with Garvey the brains, he suspected — were dangerous as a pair of rattlers. He'd guessed wrong about their intentions once, and his bad guess had cost Troop's life. Next time, it might be Jory or Laurie. He couldn't afford to take that chance.

"Thanks," he said again. He weighed the Spencer in his hand, then thrust it into the boot on his saddle. "Look after the bay," he told Culver. "He's had a long night."

He turned away and left the blacksmith standing there. At the door of the stable, he drew his Navy Colt and checked its cylinder. He holstered it again, feeling it seat smoothly in the polished leather. Then he settled the gun belt more solidly about his hips and stepped out into the street.

The distance to the stage stand seemed endless. Things were moving with the same frozen motion Merritt remembered from the War, and every detail of the morning seemed almost painfully clear to him. A farm wagon rumbled past, raising a veil of dust that hung golden in the still air. The storekeeper called a greeting from his porch, but Merritt never heard it. His eyes, his mind, all his senses, were sharpening,

276

coming to a focus on the sagging wooden door of Ma Sullivan's place.

He was still twenty paces short of that door when it opened. Adam Garvey came out, throwing a final word back over his shoulder to someone inside. Garvey laughed and pulled the door shut. He was clean-shaven, Merritt noted coldly, and he'd changed clothes somewhere after crawling around in the brush. Seeing him today, nobody would suspect he'd been out in the night doing murder. Nobody but Merritt.

Without looking Merritt's way, Garvey turned to cross the street toward the marshal's office. He paused in the middle to let a couple of riders pass. When they were gone, the street behind him was clear, empty for the moment of people and wagons and animals. Merritt smiled to himself and took a step forward.

"Adam Garvey," he called.

"Yeah. Who's that?"

Garvey broke stride, peering back into the sun. His voice showed a hint of annoyance, and the glare of the sun or his bad temper screwed his face into an impatient frown. He shaded his eyes with his hand.

"What do you—?" he began. Then he recognized Merritt.

In that instant, Garvey's face changed. The contemptuous assurance dropped from him like a cloak. His eyes showed wide and frightened in a face gone fish-belly white. Without seeming to realize it, he put out a hand as though to ward Merritt off.

"No – you can't be here." The voice was a hoarse whisper. "You're–"

Garvey stopped in time, his eyes darting swiftly right and left as his mind began to work again. Merritt stepped toward him and to the left, putting the heavy log wall of the stage stand at his back to take care of any stray bullets. Garvey watched the move and swallowed, his eyes showing a sick understanding.

"I'm what?" Merritt asked softly. "Dead?" He took another step and planted his feet. "Not today. You should've made sure at your ambush last night. The Reb Army should've taught you that, Sergeant."

"Hey, listen," Garvey said. He was recovering now, trying to act naturally, though he seemed little less afraid than when he'd first seen Merritt. "I don't know what you're talking about. You've got me wrong." He licked his lips, a quick, snakelike dart of his tongue. "We can go to the marshal and straighten this out in just a minute."

Merritt laughed. "Go to Frank?" he asked. "No, thanks. I think we can straighten things out right here. You're pretty good from ambush, or beating up an old man. Let's see how you'll do against somebody that can see you."

Two men were coming up the boardwalk, deep in conversation. Glancing up, one of them saw Merritt and Garvey ahead in the street. He broke off what he was saying and pulled up short, stretching out a hand to hold back his companion.

"Hey, what's the idea—?" the second man began. Then he took in the situation and began to back away.

Garvey's eyes darted to the men. "Get the deputy. Get Frank," he said. "The Yank's gone crazy. We need a lawman, 'fore he kills somebody."

"Too late," Merritt told him. "You had your chances to bushwhack me, you and Baldy. Now you'd better reach for your gun."

Garvey shook his head violently. "Not me," he said, the words aimed not at Merritt but at the spectators. "I never done anything to you, Yank, and I don't know why you're so hell-bent to fight. I ain't going to draw on you."

"You'd better," Merritt repeated softly. "That was Billy Troop you killed last night."

Merritt saw the change in Garvey's eyes, the shocked comprehension. Then the killer was diving to one side, his body curled small, his hand snatching cat-quick for his holstered pistol.

Merritt had been ready. He started his own draw less than a heartbeat after Garvey. Still in the same nightmare slowness, he felt the familiar weight of the Navy Colt settle into his hand. He brought it up, his arm as rigid as if this were a dueling ground. Garvey was on one knee, the muzzle of his pistol training on Merritt, his left hand sweeping across to fan the hammer. Foolish, Merritt thought in that fraction of a moment — scared, and that wouldn't help his accuracy — nothing to worry about — one shot where you want it, no matter—

Garvey's pistol roared once, and splinters from the rough logs behind him raked Merritt's cheek. The second shot was lower, still wide, slamming into the wall someplace to the left. Before there could be a third, the long barrel of the Navy Colt came to bear and Merritt squeezed the trigger.

The impact of the slug drove Garvey backward and around. He almost went headlong in the street, put out a hand to steady himself, lurched upright to a kneeling position. He looked at the pistol he still held, his face showing a mild wonder. Raising his eyes to Merritt's, he opened his mouth to speak. No words came, only a thin rill of blood that flowed down his chin and spattered over the front of his vest. He made one effort to raise the gun, and then pitched forward on his face in the dusty street.

Still poised with the Colt's hammer back for a second shot, Merritt moved up to Garvey's motionless form. He kicked the six-gun away from the outstretched hand, knelt for a second beside the body. When he straightened, he eased the hammer down but kept the gun in his hand. He'd expected to feel some sort of satisfaction — satisfaction at avenging Troop's death, at settling with Garvey once and for all. Instead, he felt only a dull weariness. It wasn't over, he knew. He still had Frank to deal with, and then there was the town.

"What's happened?" People from the stage stand and the other buildings were gathering in the street, staring at Garvey's body and at Merritt. "I heard shooting. What's it all about? Homer, did you see what happened?"

"The Yank shot Adam Garvey. Called him out pretty as you please."

"The Yank? Bad blood there. Where's the marshal? Somebody get Marshal Bell."

Less than a minute had passed since the first shot. Merritt shook himself. He heard the voices — there was a crowd by now — but their words didn't really register. He was looking across to the marshal's office.

A few seconds later, the door burst open. Frank Harmon came out on the run. Merritt stepped clear of the crowd and stood facing him, the Colt held level at his waist.

"That's far enough, Frank."

The deputy skidded to a stop thirty yards away. His eyes took in Merritt, the gun in his hand, the dead man on the ground. Frank started a move toward his own holster, but checked it immediately. Instead, he hooked his thumbs in his belt and stood facing Merritt.

"What's the gun for, Yank?" His voice was hoarse at first, but gathered strength as he went along. "There's a fine for shooting in town. Better put it away."

"He killed Garvey," somebody called from the front rank of the crowd. They had split now, backing away from the two men, but still near enough to see the next act. Most of the town was here by now. Merritt saw the storekeeper, Mr. Evans, and Cap Daingerfield from the saloon, and a dozen other familiar faces. "Shot him dead. I'd say we ought to string him up."

A buzz of voices ran around the watchers, some approving, some not. Neither Merritt nor Frank reacted to them. The deputy took a step forward, then another.

"I knew that gun would get you in trouble, Yank. I'm arresting you. If you don't want to make it worse, you'll come in peaceable."

Despite himself, Merritt felt a grudging admiration for Frank's nerve. Shaken as he must have been by his partner's death and Merritt's reappearance, he was still determined to play out his string. Garvey might have been the brains of the group, but the deputy had obviously supplied the guts.

"You killed Billy Troop," Merritt said quietly. "You and Garvey. When the marshal gets back—"

"You've just shot one of our citizens, Yank. Maybe you figure you can get away with it by some cock-and-bull story, but you can't. Hand over that gun, before these good folks decide to lynch you."

"Ain't no deciding about it," Cap Daingerfield yelled. He shoved forward. "Let's get him, boys."

Scattered voices shouted their agreement. Two or three of the crowd began to elbow their way toward Merritt. He raised the pistol and they halted as though they'd been turned to stone.

"Stand easy. I'll shoot if I have to."

"Who'll you shoot, Yank?" Frank asked. He took another step, stopped when the muzzle of the Navy Colt swung toward him. "You gonna kill us all, the way you killed Garvey? I figure you only have four or five more rounds."

283

"That's right." Merritt moved back until his shoulders brushed the solid wall. He kept the gun steady on Frank. "You'll get the first one, though. The marshal's on his way back right now, with the whole story. We'll just wait for him."

As soon as the words were out, Merritt knew he'd made a mistake. Frank's smile disappeared and his mouth set in a hard line. He knew now that he didn't have much time. He scanned the faces in the crowd, and his voice came out sharp and authoritative.

"Cap. Willie. Gil Stratton. Sid Culver. You're deputized. Fan out behind me. If he makes a move to get away, shoot him."

"Wait a minute, Frank," the blacksmith said. He took a hesitant step forward and looked around uneasily. "He said something about Billy Troop being shot. I think we better wait for Marshal Bell and let him figure this out."

But the crowd was already edging away, and the three others named had ranged themselves behind Frank. The deputy looked at Culver, but spoke to the whole group.

"I just want him disarmed, Sid. You ain't gonna leave an armed killer running loose while we check his story, are you? He'll be safe in jail until the marshal gets back."

"He's lying," Merritt snapped. "He and

Garvey are the killers. They bushwhacked Billy, and they almost killed Tom Drake. I'm not giving up my gun to him."

Culver's troubled gaze went from Merritt to the deputy and back. Merritt knew he wasn't convincing the listening crowd. He was still the outsider, and Frank was one of them.

"Be better if you gave up, Yank," Culver said at last. "We'll see nobody hurts you. I want to know what happened to Billy."

Merritt knew he'd lost. He shook his head a trifle, and Culver stepped back, moving to join the line of deputies flanking Frank. "You be careful, Henry Simpson," a woman called from the boardwalk. Somebody snickered, but the man moved to take his place beside the others, hand on the butt of his pistol. More men from the crowd joined him, so that almost a dozen now faced Merritt, waiting for Frank to give them their lead.

For an instant, Merritt wished for the Spencer. With that in his hand, he could clear out this nest of Rebs, and—

And nothing, his mind finished. "You can't win a gunfight here," Bell had told him long ago. Now he saw that the marshal was right. He couldn't see the men backing Frank as enemies, as if the War was still on. They were the solid backbone of the town. Now they were standing up for the law, and if shooting started, some of them were going to be killed.

"I'll still get you first, Frank," Merritt said. But he wasn't quite sure, and Frank must have felt it. The deputy waved back his men.

"Don't go for your guns unless he shoots. We want him alive." He stepped toward Merritt, holding out his left hand. His right dropped slowly toward the butt of his holstered pistol. "Give it up, Yank. Tell you what, you give up your iron, and I'll give up mine. Sid can hold them until the marshal comes. That's fair, ain't it?"

Merritt knew it was a trick. Even if he made the deal, the look on the faces of Cap Daingerfield and his friends was enough to show it would never be kept. He'd end up stretching rope on a cottonwood down by the river, and Frank would have at least a chance of getting away clean. The best choice he had was to take the deputy with him — and from the growing confidence in Frank's eyes, even that was slipping away.

"Get your hand away from your holster," Merritt said tightly. "We wait for Bell, or we both go out together."

"I'm just telling you, I'll hand over my gun," Frank said. He was only a few steps away now. Too softly for the others to hear, he murmured,

"Think you can cock that Colt and get me before I have time to draw, Yank? I'll bet you can't."

"It's not a good bet, Frank."

The deputy shrugged. "It's the only one I have left." He set his feet, his eyes steady on Merritt. "Get ready, Yank."

"Stand where you are! Nobody move!"

In spite of the order, heads swiveled in the direction of the voice. Marshal Bell stood on the boardwalk on the far side of the street, a shotgun held at his waist. He jerked the muzzle of it at Frank's makeshift posse.

"Clear that street, before I forget my manners. Henry, you ought to know better. You're too old for this foolishness. Everybody else just stand still."

"Good to see you, Marshal," Frank said. "The Yank shot Garvey and tried to tree the town. Looks like he's gone plumb crazy. We just—"

His voice died away. Jim Bob Drake had stepped from the alley beside the saloon to stand with the marshal. Frank licked his lips and squared around so he could see both Bell and Merritt.

"Clear that street, I said. Move!"

Under the lash of Bell's tongue, the onlookers were drifting back into doorways and alleys. Merritt and the deputy stood alone now.

"Mr. Merritt, you holster that Colt and step away."

Merritt obeyed. Frank's eyes followed him.

"Now." Bell stepped down from the rough planks into the street. "All right, Frank. I want your gun. Your badge, too."

"I reckon not, Marshal."

"Son, don't try it. Nobody beats a scatter-gun."

Frank Harmon laughed. "Nobody beats a rope, either," he said, and his hand flashed for his gun.

In the same instant, Merritt moved. This time, it was different. He'd thought Garvey was fast, but Harmon was a professional, a man who made his living with his gun. The deputy must have seen him start his draw, because he pivoted smoothly away from Bell. Merritt's Colt still stood in leather when the black muzzle of Frank's pistol came up on his chest. Frank was grinning crazily, his mouth opening in a shout of anger and triumph.

The shotgun roared. A blast of pellets swept Frank off his feet, rolling him across the board-walk until his body fetched up with a thump against the wall of the stage stand. His pistol still only half out, Merritt stared down at the crumpled body until Bell caught his arm and shook him.

"You hit? I thought he'd got you."

"No." Merritt carefully returned the Colt to its holster. "I'm all right, I guess."

Bell snorted. "I told you about playing lawman. You better learn it, or that woman of yours will be out another man."

"Don't worry. I think I learned."

Bell turned away and bent over Frank. After a few seconds, he straightened.

"Nasty thing, a shotgun." He turned it in his hands, then leaned it carefully against the wall. Standing over Frank's body, he shook his head.

"Too bad. Best deputy I ever had," he said. He looked at Merritt. "A good man with a gun."

CHAPTER 19

The circuit preacher was a frail-looking old man, his thin bony shoulders seeming bowed beneath the weight of his black frock coat. He stood beside Clint's grave, sharp eyes roving over the little gathering in Gilead's cemetery. He looked as if he could deliver a real hell-and-damnation sermon, Merritt thought, but when the old man opened his limp black Bible, he chose one of the psalms.

"Give thanks unto the Lord, for he is good," he read in a strong voice. "For his mercy endureth for ever."

It seemed a strange beginning for a funeral service, but Merritt found he couldn't keep his mind on the sermon that followed. His eyes strayed first to the new white headstone — "Clinton Ashley Davidson, 1831-1867," the inscription read, with a verse and a carved wreath — and then to the handful of mourners who had climbed the low hill to the burying ground.

Laurie stood beside him, slim and silent in black, a veil hiding her face. Jory clung to her hand. He wore his new Sunday suit — already showing wear at the knees — and his mouth was set in a straight line with the effort of not crying. Marshal Bell was there, along with Sid Culver and the Evanses and Banker Whitlock. Farther back, Houston and Zack Allgood fidgeted uncomfortably, and beneath a big oak that grew by the cemetery gate, Tom Drake and Jim Bob stood with bared heads.

With Drake's help, Merritt and the marshal had located Clint's body, dumped in a shallow grave below the fort. The idea of a formal burial was the marshal's — "Nothing like a tombstone to set folks' minds at rest," he'd said — but Merritt agreed. Eastward from the hilltop lay Gilead, with the stage road threading south toward the low bulk of Phantom Hill. To the west was the river and the endless tossing grass of the buffalo plains. It was the sort of place Clint would've liked.

"Let us pray," the minister said at last. Afterward, he shuffled down to murmur a few words to Laurie, and then it was finished. The circuit rider went off for supper with the Evanses, and the others drifted back down the steep wagon track toward town. Laurie stayed behind, still looking down at the mounded grave.

"Laurie," Merritt began. Then he felt a touch on his arm and turned to see Marshal Bell. The lawman drew him aside.

"Stop by my office directly, son, if you will," Bell said. "We still have some business to finish."

"Sure, Marshal. It may be a little while, though."

"No hurry. I figure on a drink or two first. Never did care for funerals." He looked past Merritt toward Laurie, and his lips quirked. "Next time you get her in front of a preacher, I hope it's for a different reason."

He stumped off down the hill, and Merritt turned again to Laurie.

"We'd better go," he said, taking her arm gently.

She didn't move. "It's really over now," she said. Her voice was husky with tears. "I didn't think I'd cry. I've been sure he was dead for months. It just never seemed − real − before." She looked up at him miserably. "I'm sorry, Steve."

"There's nothing to be sorry about. I know how you felt about Clint − and how he felt about you."

She stood very still for a second longer, then put back the veil and began to dry her eyes. "Jory?" She looked around. "He's wandered off again."

"He won't go far."

"I guess not." She turned away from him, shading her eyes to look out across the plains. "He asked last night if you were going away now. Are you?"

Merritt stepped up behind her, resting his hands on her shoulders. "Don't you know?" he asked.

"I'd like to hear it."

"Guess I'd better stay," he said. He laughed softly. "Marshal Bell wants me to make an honest woman of you. How does that sound?"

She turned to face him, and her eyes were clear and level now, the way they'd looked when he first saw her.

"I'd like that," she said seriously. "I'd like to be an honest woman with you."

"Laur-iee!" Grace Evans was down by the gate of the cemetery, one plump hand cupped by her mouth. "Laurie, you all come down to supper with us and the reverend. Bring the Ya— Mr. Merritt, too."

"Oh." Laurie looked around, startled. "I'd forgotten Jory. We'd better—"

"Go ahead." Merritt shepherded her gently toward the older woman. "I'll find him. I think I know where to look."

His guess was right. He found the boy standing in the deep shade beside the place they'd laid Billy Troop. A small bunch of yellow flowers lay on the raw earth of the mound. A busy carpet spider was weaving its web at the base of the stone while Jory watched.

"Hello, Jory," Merritt said. "Are you all right?"

The boy nodded, his face turned away. Merritt squatted beside him. For a long time, neither spoke. Then Jory said, "I miss him. He taught me a lot."

"Me, too," Merritt said. He put his hand on the boy's shoulder. "Jory, your ma's waiting for us, but first I need to see the marshal. Will you walk along with me?"

Jory looked up at him. After a moment, he smiled. "Sure, Yank," he said.

Bell was at his desk, the pieces of his old revolver spread out before him. He ruffled Jory's hair when the boy came over to watch.

"Seemed like a good time to clean it," he said to Merritt. "Never any trouble in town right after a funeral."

"I didn't think the town noticed." Merritt's voice showed more bitterness than he'd intended. "Not many of them turned up."

Bell held up the pistol's cylinder and squinted at it critically. "Give them a chance, boy," he said. "These folks liked Frank, and they tolerated Garvey and Baldy easy enough. What happened will take some getting over, but I don't think you'll have any more trouble."

"I don't think so either." Merritt spread his hands. "I didn't mean that. The fault hasn't been all theirs."

Bell's approving glance shifted to Merritt for a second, and then he began assembling the Colt, his square hands surprisingly nimble.

"Jory, hand me that there spring – that's it." He paused, came back to Merritt. "One thing, son. That night Jim Bob Drake came after me, he told me some wild story about his pa and Rebels and gold and Clint's killing. You know about all that?"

"I know."

"Um. Surprised you ain't dug up that gold by now."

Merritt laughed harshly. "There isn't any gold." He turned to the window, looking out into Gilead's dusty street.

"I talked to my friend in the Yankee Army, Marshal. He did some checking for me. While he was following those Rebs down from Kansas, another column was coming from the east to cut them off." He turned, rested his hands on the desk. "That column was camped at Phantom Hill. The Rebs never got there. The Comanches caught up first, and your gold is

295

someplace out on the plains — for whoever wants it."

The marshal took some time to think about that. "Well," he said at last, "that pretty much leaves it up to you. There's nobody else alive to press charges against Tom Drake — assuming I believed that fool story."

Merritt stood in silence for a full minute. Then, finally, he began to laugh. "I think Jim Bob took you in, Marshal," he said. "You know how kids are, these days."

Bell nodded. "That's good," he said. "That's just what I thought. You all run along now."

Merritt gathered up Jory and turned to the door, but Bell's soft question stopped him.

"Yank? Those Southern boys at Cedar Creek — did they fight good?"

Looking back at Bell, Merritt remembered it all again — the surprise, the charge by Early's howling army, all that he'd seen that day. But it was a long time ago, and now there were more important things.

"They fought good, Marshal," he said. "The best I ever saw."

As they left the office, Jory tugged impatiently at Merritt's sleeve. "Steve? Was that in the War?" he demanded. "Tell me about it!"

Merritt shook his head. "No, Jory," he said. "The War's over."

He dropped an arm around the boy's shoulders. Together, they walked up the street toward the house where Laurie was waiting.

THORNDIKE PRESS HOPES you have enjoyed this Large Print book. All our Large Print titles are designed for the easiest reading, and all our books are made to last. Other Thorndike Press Large Print books are available at your library, through selected bookstores, or directly from the publisher. For more information about current and upcoming titles, please call us, toll free, at 1-800-223-6121, or mail your name and address to:

THORNDIKE PRESS
P. O. BOX 159
THORNDIKE, MAINE 04986

There is no obligation, of course.